KIT MEETS COVINGTON

Bobbi JG Weiss

CANDLEWICK
ENTERTAINMENT

Chapter 1

A LEAP OF FAITH

Whoa! Kit Bridges thought as the plane dipped slightly, sending her stomach into yet another uncomfortable spasm. Flying didn't bother her much, but turbulence? She could do without turbulence, especially today. Today, her life seemed to be nothing *but* turbulence. *Well, yeah, but it's a* good *turbulence,* she told herself, clutching a brochure in her fist.

She had been holding that brochure since she'd started her journey from Great Falls International Airport, in Montana. From there she had arrived safely at JFK, in New York City, where she had checked her luggage, waited two hours, and boarded the huge British Airways Airbus A380 jet. Now here she sat, hurtling across the Atlantic Ocean at a bazillion miles an hour and still clutching the brochure as if her life depended on it.

THE COVINGTON ACADEMY
FOR THE
EQUESTRIAN ARTS

That's what the brochure said, and that's where she was headed: The Covington Academy, in England, yes, *England*, which was almost five thousand miles away from—well, away from what used to be home. All it took was a couple of flights, and *bammo*, she'd be at a new school in a new country, living a whole new life!

The person in the seat next to her gave a loud snore. Kit couldn't help but giggle. Her father, Rudy, always snored when he napped. Usually he was pretty quiet about it, breathing deeply through his nose and only snuffling a little. But every now and then he'd let out a big honker like that one.

Kit peeked under the brown Stetson hat that covered his face to find that he was still deeply asleep. How in the world could he sleep at a time like this? Their lives were turning upside down even at this very moment, and he was snoring! That was Rudy all over, as mellow as a mountain sunset, a cool, calm cowboy through and through.

Maybe it was time for her to catch a few winks, too. Kit's emotions had been seesawing between excitement and terror for days now. Sometimes she couldn't really tell if she was feeling good or bad about all the changes taking place—both feelings put equal butterflies in her stomach. *Oh c'mon, change is good,* she told herself, *especially after everything that's happened this past year. It's just what you need. And Dad needs it even more, though he'll always be the last one to admit it.*

She settled back in her seat and tried to relax, letting her mind wander. Not surprisingly, it wandered directly to Charlie, the friend she was leaving behind. She missed him so much already! She and Charlie were the same age: fourteen. They went to the same school, liked the same music, craved the same junk food, and even wore the same fashion style: boho chic.

Kit's hand drifted to the necklace she was wearing, a going-away present from Charlie, who had announced that it was a "black suede crescent bolo tie with a handcrafted sterling silver lucky horseshoe adornment." Charlie knew the precise terms for everything, from fashion styles to sports equipment. He had even been there when she'd picked out her new favorite sweater, a long purplish knit number from a thrift store. She was wearing it right now to top off her travel ensemble: layered shirts, blue jeans, a coarsely woven blue scarf with cute little bug-eyed owls on it, and her floppy red felt hat.

Kit wasn't a fashion nut, but she had her own unique look.

If only I could call Charlie, or even just zip him a text, she thought, peeved that the airline didn't allow passengers to use cell phones. *Then I'd feel better.*

She and Charlie had made up a game called Best/Worst that they played whenever one of them had to face a difficult situation. Kit imagined Charlie sitting next to her now and asking, "Okay, Kit-Cat, Best/Worst. What's the worst thing that could happen when you get to Covington?"

Hmm, Kit thought. *The worst thing would be that I'd hate it, but I don't think I will. I think I'll really like it.*

"Then what's the best thing that could happen when you get to Covington?" imaginary Charlie asked.

I'll absolutely love it, Kit thought, then realized, *Hey, both answers are good!* Smiling, she relaxed her grip on the brochure and closed her eyes.

Time slipped away. She wasn't sure how much, but suddenly she felt like she was back on her dad's ranch, riding her old horse, Freckles. He was a small Appaloosa, a gentle soul that she used to ride every chance she got. As he happily carried her along Streamside Trail, she basked in the summer sun, enjoying the heady scent of flowers in bloom while songbirds trilled in the brush and—

Chaos! the world twisting and whirling, a horrible cracking pain in her foot, and drums, drums, the thunderclap of drums beating loud, so loud, so loud in her head, *so many drums and pain and fear, and HER HEAD WAS GOING TO EXPLODE AND*—

"Cuppa, miss?"

Kit jolted awake. *What? Where am I? Who*—*?*

She found herself staring up at one of the flight attendants, who wore a crisp blue uniform with a cute tufted cravat and jaunty cap. "Didn't mean to startle you, young lady. Just wondering . . ." The woman gestured to her drinks cart in the narrow aisle. "Nothing like a hot cuppa to soothe the nerves, no?"

She spoke in an English accent like most of the other airline personnel Kit had met that day, though Kit heard another accent blended in, maybe Jamaican. "I'm sorry, a cup of what?" she asked, covering a yawn.

The flight attendant grinned. "Just a cuppa," she said. "That's what we British folk call a cup of tea." She was clearly used to explaining British terms to American travelers.

"Oh." Kit rubbed her eyes and straightened in her seat. "Um . . . I've never had tea, actually. I'm a coffee girl, like my dad." She pointed to the softly snoring Stetson beside her.

"Well," said the woman, "I think it's about time you try some then, no?"

"I'm game." Kit figured she should learn to drink the stuff if she was going to live in England. She had always heard how much British people loved tea, and she didn't want to look like a totally hopeless newbie. "With milk and sugar, please," she said. "That's the way I like coffee, so chances are it's the way I'll like tea, right?"

"There's only one way to find out." The attendant picked up a plastic teacup and saucer from a stack on her cart and reached for the milk pitcher. "A bit of advice," she said. "The secret to a really good cup of tea is to put the milk in first." She did so, then added hot tea from a kettle.

Kit accepted the now-steaming cup and its saucer.

The flight attendant noticed the school brochure, which Kit had placed on her seatback tray. "That's The Covington Academy, isn't it?"

"Yeah." Kit set her tea on the tray. "My dad got a new job there, and I'll be a new student. A full scholarship and everything. Pretty cool, huh?"

"You must be one fine student," said the attendant, offering Kit a few packets of sugar.

"Er, not really," Kit admitted. The attendant raised an eyebrow at this, but Kit said quickly, "How do you know about Covington?"

"My nephew, he goes to Tonbridge, a boys' school in Kent," she replied. "He's one competitive rider, he is. I go to his shows whenever my schedule allows. Watch out, you may meet him in the arena someday."

Only if I compete, Kit thought, but she didn't say it out loud. The issue of her riding at Covington was going to be its own kettle of fish, as her dad phrased it. Not knowing what else to say, she added sugar to her tea, stirred, and took a sip. "Hey, this is pretty good," she said, smacking her lips. "Way different from coffee, but good."

"You've cleared your first hurdle then, so to speak." The attendant chuckled at her equestrian pun and began to push her cart farther down the aisle to tend to the next passengers. "Oh, it's Earl Grey, by the way." She indicated Kit's cup. "The tea."

"Oh, right. Thanks." Kit took another sip. *Whoever you are, Mr. Grey, you make totally delish tea.*

And tea was just the beginning, Kit was sure of it. She was going to reach England in a few hours, and life there was going to be good. Better than good. Life was going to be fantastic! *I don't know how,* she thought, gazing at the Covington brochure, *but I'm totally gonna rock this!*

Chapter 2

OUT OF THE GATE

By the time the plane landed at Heathrow Airport in London, Kit wondered if she'd skipped the whole *another country* thing and gone straight to *another planet.*

To begin with, the minute she stood up from her seat, her legs went all wobbly as if the force of gravity had doubled. Her feet were so numbed out, it was like they weren't there. Her poor rear end tingled horribly from a major attack of pins and needles, and everything sounded muffled, as if somebody had wrapped her head in a horse blanket. She knew it was because she'd been sitting for so long in a noisy jet, but that didn't quite explain it. Everything felt different somehow. Not bad but just . . . weird, though she couldn't say exactly why.

She heard her father's wry chuckle. "Hey," she grunted, "stop laughing at me."

"Then quit being so funny," Rudy grunted right back at her. He steadied her as she wobbled out of the plane, through the connecting walkway, and into the terminal, where they spent way too much time collecting their luggage, going through customs, and finding a cab. Kit's senses had a chance to slowly balance out, though, and after grabbing a quick pastry snack for energy, father and daughter embarked on the last leg of their journey: the drive from London to The Covington Academy itself.

"Oh, my gosh, this is going to be so great, Dad!" Kit enthused as their driver took them out of the city and into the English countryside. "I know we've both been totally freaking out, but change is good." She'd been convincing herself to believe it for days. Now that she was actually in England, she did believe it!

The pastry's sugar jolt helped.

Rudy stared out the window. "I am not freaking out," he assured her in a tone that said exactly the opposite.

Kit couldn't resist saying, "You're wearing your lucky flannel."

Rudy glanced down at his blue-checked flannel shirt. He wasn't the kind of guy who really believed in luck, yet he did think of the shirt as his "lucky flannel." Go figure.

"Don't worry, Dad. You are going to be the best chief equestrian supervisor England has ever seen!"

Rudy sighed. "It just all happened so fast. First the mystery package in the mail . . ."

"The phone call where we couldn't understand a word the lady was saying!" Kit laughed. "And now we're here! The Covington Academy! A fancy new school for me, a stable full of horses for you—it's a win-win!" When her father didn't respond, Kit knew why. The sadness in his eyes broke her heart. "Mom would be so psyched that we're doing this," she told him softly.

He nodded. "She always did want to bring us to England."

"The country she grew up in," Kit said, gazing out the window. *And what a country it is!* she thought. She had always considered her family's little corner of northern Montana to be a land of green mountains, green trees, and rolling meadows full of wild green grass, but compared to England? It didn't compare.

The English countryside practically exploded green in every direction. Even the barriers that separated the countless plots of land were green. Hedgerows, they were called—long rows of bushes and trees instead of wooden fencing. *Even the dirt looks green!* Kit thought, giggling to herself. Of course the dirt wasn't green. It was brown, like regular old dirt. Yet to her eyes, there was an unusual quality to it that she'd never seen before, a deep richness that spoke of frequent rain and wind and thick morning fog. *It's alien dirt,* she thought, *but not for long. This dirt is about to become home turf!*

"So." Rudy draped an arm around Kit's shoulders. "Equestrian academy. Does this mean you might actually get on a horse?"

"Not a chance, Rudy. I'm sure it's not like *everyone* rides. There's probably a ton of other stuff to do."

Rudy rolled his eyes. "It's *Dad,*" he drawled, "and will you promise me that you'll at least consider it? Remember—"

Kit knew what was coming next, so she recited her dad's favorite saying along with him: "If you haven't fallen off a horse, you haven't ridden long enough."

"Everyone falls off, kiddo," Rudy added.

Kit just frowned. "Not like that," she muttered. Her thoughts turned dark, dark enough to bring her mood crashing down.

And then she saw it: her new school. "Holy cow!" Any further words got stuck in her throat as their cab turned off the country road and onto an enormous gravel driveway. The cabbie brought them right up to the front door of the main building.

Her mouth hanging open, Kit fumbled her way out of the cab. "Rudy," she finally said, "this place is like a castle!"

"Kit," her father pleaded, "stop calling me Rudy."

A familiar rumble in the earth made Kit turn just as several students in slick riding uniforms rode by on smartly groomed horses, their hooves clattering against the gravel. They were followed by a young man running and waving his arms wildly. "Circle wide, left flank!" he yelled to several other boys with him. "Move, move, move!"

Rudy's cowboy instincts kicked in. "They need help," he told Kit. "Stay here!"

The riders who had just passed dismounted and ran back to offer assistance as the ground rumbled again. Something huge and black thundered out of nowhere and rushed straight at Kit.

I just got here, and now I'm gonna die! Kit thought, too terrified to move.

"Watch out!" Somebody grabbed her and pulled her safely to one side.

Kit barely noticed her savior. All she could do was gape as a beautiful black horse reared up with a wild rebel whinny, his front hooves pawing the air right where she'd been standing. He had no rider and no saddle or bridle. Kit figured he must have escaped the stables. She watched, mesmerized, as the horse pranced first one way then the other, trying to find a path to freedom through the ring of humans slowly closing around him. Kit barely heard her dad's soft voice calmly issuing instructions to the students so that they could safely capture the animal.

"Sorry," came another voice, much closer and very much louder. Kit whirled around to find herself face-to-face with her savior, a handsome . . . very handsome . . . young man with an expression of concern on his face. "I didn't mean to startle you," he said. "I just wanted to make sure I got you out of the way in time."

"Wh-what was that?" Kit managed to ask.

Seeing that she was all right, he relaxed. "Covington's wildest resident. He's impossible to tame. I'm surprised they haven't shipped him off."

The young man's unusual accent finally pulled Kit out of her daze. She looked at him properly and almost did a double take. "Are you for real? You look just like a guy from those old movies, the ones I watch for school instead of reading the book!" She felt a silly grin spread across her face. He was really cute. Really. *Really.*

The young man grinned back. "I'm Nav Andrada. I haven't seen you before. Are you new to Covington?"

"Oh, uh, Kit Bridges." Kit stuck out her hand. Nav shook it in welcome while beaming an utterly charming smile at her. His suave manner only made her feel awkward. *Oh, yeah, I'm as new to Covington as you can get,* she thought, saying aloud, "What was your first clue?"

Nav chuckled. "Don't worry. The first day of school is overwhelming for all of us. Once you're sorted, we shall go out for a ride. *Hasta luego,* Kit Bridges." He sauntered away, leaving Kit stunned all over again. *Castles and wild beasts and knights in tailored suits who rescue clueless maidens,* she thought, trying to make sense of all the weirdness around her.

"Are you all right, Kit?" Rudy asked, rejoining her while one of the boys led the recaptured gelding back toward the stable.

Kit was still reeling from what Nav had said: *we shall go for a ride. . . .* "Yeah, but Dad, you may have been right. I think every single person here rides. And did you see that crazy horse?"

"Should we make a run for it?" Rudy asked.

For a split second, Kit actually took the question seriously, probably because her heart was still pounding. But to leave? Now? "No way! We're the Bridges. We can totally do this. Check it." She turned to the main school building. "We live in a castle now!"

"Watch your back!"

Kit spun around to see the black gelding loose again, and again he was heading right for her. "On second thought," she told her dad, "*run!*"

She and Rudy bolted through their new castle's front door.

Chapter 3

FIRST IMPRESSIONS

Dad, that horse was coming straight at me," Kit panted once they were inside. "Me!" She didn't know what to think. It was as if the animal had picked her out of the crowd on purpose. Twice!

Rudy took his daughter's reaction in stride. "Glad to see you didn't lose your flair for the dramatic on the flight over, Kit." He took off his Stetson and surveyed the school's main lobby.

Kit turned in circles, gawking at everything. She felt like she was in a museum or on a fancy movie set. Huge paintings of horses framed in elaborate gold hung on the walls. There were enough decorative wooden moldings and panels to build another whole building. Students, parents, and teachers milled about, their footwear clicking and clacking sharply against the pristine wood-and-tile flooring. There were bright, colorful flowers in fancy vases on every table, lush potted ferns in decorative plant stands, and not a speck of dust on any surface that she could see.

"Holy queen of England, look at this place!" Kit glanced up. "Hey, put me on your shoulders so I can take a selfie with the chandelier."

"I'm not sure that's your best idea," said Rudy.

"I thought we were risk takers, thrill seekers," she teased. "England's already changed you."

"Which way now, do you think?" At a loss, Rudy sought help from the nearest student. "Excuse me, could you point us in the direction of the dining hall?"

A girl already wearing the school uniform looked up from her campus map, her dark eyes wide with confusion. At the sight of Rudy's Stetson, she squeaked, "Oh!" followed by, "I haven't the slightest! I'm totally turned around!" As if to demonstrate, she turned the map in her hands sideways, then around again as if it might make more sense upside down. "Uhhh . . ." She pointed. "That way! Oh wait, no, that's where I got lost last time. It's definitely not that way. Um . . ." After another check of her map, she admitted, "Oh, I'm sorry." She shrugged. "Good luck!"

Kit gave her an understanding smile. "You, too," she said as she followed her dad down a random hallway. She faintly heard the poor girl ask the throngs of nearby students: "Did anybody just see a *cowboy?*"

Kit was impressed when the first door Rudy chose to walk through took them to the dining hall. A young woman behind the student registration table rose from her chair. "Welcome! You must be the Bridges."

Kit muffled a laugh. *Dad might as well be wearing a sign that says* HUG ME, I'M A COWBOY.

"I'm Sally Warrington," the woman continued. "I'm a teacher, and I work with the headmistress. Now, Mr. Bridges—"

"Call me Rudy."

"Oh, um." Sally gave a flustered little laugh. "I wouldn't dare."

Kit exchanged an amused glance with her dad. There was no doubt in either of their minds that Sally Warrington was a very proper English lady. She was also rather like a bird—colorfully dressed and very pretty, with a sweet, fragile quality that made Kit wonder how strict she could possibly be about enforcing school rules. Not too strict, Kit hoped.

"Now, Mr. Bridges," Sally said, "I'm sure you'll want to see the stables and your quarters straightaway. Katherine, I'll show you the way to Rose Cottage, your new home."

"Call me Kit," Kit said immediately. "I go by Kit."

Sally smiled and gestured. "Shall we?"

"Right." Rudy faced Kit square on. "I guess this is where we split up."

Kit realized she wasn't ready for this. She wasn't ready to go it alone, not yet. "We're kind of a team, Miss Warrington. Could I hang with him just a bit longer?"

"How charming," Sally said in delight. "We do like rules and order at Covington, but perhaps we can be a touch flexible today. *Only* for today, mind."

Kit happily slipped her arm through her dad's. Excellent. It looked like Sally Warrington was the understanding type.

"Even the horses live in castles!" That was the first thing Rudy said when he got a look at the school stables.

Kit couldn't agree more. This was the cleanest stable she'd ever seen. She imagined each horse having to wipe its hooves on a doormat before being allowed in. "Do you think you can get used to this?" she asked her father.

"As long as there are horses around, I'll be all right."

"Mr. Bridges." A stable hand appeared, holding a rake, apparently having just laid out new straw bedding in one of the stalls. He shook hands with Rudy. "We bin expectin' yeh."

Rudy instantly transformed into the official chief equestrian supervisor and guided the stable hand away, asking him something about training schedules. Kit didn't mind being left behind so abruptly. She knew her dad had to do his job. Instead she marveled at how cool the stable hand had sounded with his thick Scottish accent. The people here all sounded so different!

First had been their cabbie, who had spoken with what he'd called a West Midlands accent. Then there was handsome Nav with his London accent overlaying another one, maybe Portuguese? She wasn't sure. Then Miss Warrington had spoken what Kit had read was called Received Pronunciation, or RP, the kind of accent that British Broadcasting Company announcers used on TV and the radio. *They all sound so exotic!* she thought.

Her thoughts stopped dead when she glanced at the nameplate on the nearest stall: "TK." What kind of name was that for a horse? She peeked in, and to her surprise, the wild black gelding gazed back at her. "Oh, it's you again," she said.

After taking a quick look around to make sure nobody was watching, she slid the stall gate open. Even as she did so, she wondered if she'd just taken stupid pills or something. The horse was dangerous. He'd tried to gallop over her, for heaven's sake!

But something was drawing her to him. She didn't know what, but she couldn't resist it. "I just want to say hi to you, okay?" she said calmly, noting that TK was still barred from escaping his stall by a rope tied in some kind of tricky-looking slipknot. Good. "You almost gave me a heart attack earlier," she told him as he took a step forward, pressing his chest against the rope and leaning his head out toward her. "Guess you lost that round, huh? You can run really fast."

TK just stood there, so Kit slowly raised her hand and touched his muzzle. He didn't move. She began to pet him. His muzzle was soft, like velvet, and warm. She let her hand slide up to stroke his face. TK snorted, and that made Kit laugh. "You're friendlier than you look," she said, now stroking his forehead. "But you may want to try a different approach with the ladies in the future."

"You're gonna want to back away slowly," came a soft voice behind her. "He's lethal."

Kit turned to see the student who had caught TK when he'd gotten loose. She remembered that someone had called him Will. He was gesturing her away from TK, so she poked her head out of the stall and then noticed the sign on TK's door:

UNPREDICTABLE AND DANGEROUS.
KEEP GATE SHUT — HORSE WILL BOLT

She didn't believe it. "He doesn't seem so bad now," she pointed out, continuing to pet a docile TK.

Will said, "Fine, don't take my advice. I only work here." Then with more authority he ordered, "Come on!"

Kit took a few steps toward him, just to show him she wasn't entirely brain-dead. But before she could ask him more about TK, three girls in riding gear entered the stable. One had her hair in a long braid, and she was leading a chestnut Thoroughbred, patting his neck as she said to her friends, "Well, it looks like my summer memorizing the new training manual has paid off. I do enjoy ranking first."

Will was still talking to Kit. "I've already had to chase him down once today, and I really don't fancy doing it again."

Kit was so busy thinking, *Wow, this guy is cute! This school is full of cute guys!* that she didn't realize her mouth was saying something as lame as, "I thought you riding types loved running. Good conditioning or whatever."

Will stared at her. "You riding types?" he repeated in disbelief.

The girl with the braid handed her horse's reins to one of her pals and strode up to Will with bold confidence. "Hi! I've been looking everywhere for you," she said to him. Her attempt to act coy didn't quite work, as far as Kit was concerned. Will didn't seem too eager for her presence, either. "I hope your summer was as brill as mine was," the girl went on, beaming at him. "Was it?"

"Uh, yeah, it was okay," Will muttered.

"Did you see my e-mails? I kept you updated."

"Very updated."

"Well, that was the plan."

Will didn't say anything.

The girl was clearly not happy with his lack of enthusiasm, but she kept going, kind of like a dog who wouldn't give up a bone. "What's curious is that I didn't seem to receive any back. Could that be right?"

Will looked as if he'd rather have been locked in a cage full of angry cheetahs than standing next to this girl. He stared down at his boots, making vague waving motions over his face as if trying to magically erase himself.

The girl watched him for a moment. A flash of dismay crossed her features, but then she was beaming again and addressing Kit. "We haven't met. Elaine Whiltshire."

"Hi, I'm—"

"Do you ride? You're not dressed, and I didn't see you out there."

"No, I—I didn't—"

"How odd. You see, I can't announce my win until you ride." Elaine squared her shoulders as if assuming command of the world. "Tack up," she ordered Kit. "Let's see what you've got. Competitive riding is what Covington is all about and—" She stopped at the sound of a whinny and gaped at something over Kit's shoulder.

TK was lunging out of his stall!

"TK!" Will shouted, automatically pulling Kit to safety as TK trotted past, heading for the doors. Elaine had to dodge out of the way, too, and she crouched down as low as possible, clearly afraid that TK might bite or kick. He didn't, though. Once outside, he broke into a gallop, ready to lead Will on another merry chase around the school grounds.

Kit watched Will run after him, shouting, "TK, get back here!"

But he was secure, she thought. *I'm sure of it!* She turned to check.

The rope that had been tied across the doorway now lay on the straw floor. TK had untied the knot!

Kit was impressed. *That is a wickedly clever horse!* Still, his escape was her fault. She wondered if she was going to get in trouble.

Elaine straightened up from her protective crouch. She did not look pleased.

"Oh, my gosh, I am so, so sorry!" Kit cried. "It was totally my bad!"

Elaine's glare could have frozen a cup of hot tea.

In a panic of guilt, Kit snatched Elaine's riding helmet up from the floor where she'd dropped it and thrust it out. "Here's your—your hat!"

Elaine grabbed it. "It's a helmet," she snapped.

"Yeah, um . . . I don't ride."

"Yes. Well, that's become rather evident." Elaine raised her chin and glared at Kit. "If you don't ride, stay out of the stalls." And she walked briskly out of the stable.

Kit wanted to crawl into a hole.

Chapter 4

SHARING WITH ANYA

A short time later, Kit was back to gaping at the exquisite grounds of The Covington Academy—in particular, Rose Cottage, the Fourth-Form girls' dormitory.

As Sally guided Kit down the pathway leading to Rose Cottage, she explained about forms, which were the English equivalent of grades. Fourth Form in England was the equivalent of ninth grade in the United States. Sally further explained that Covington, like most English prep schools, went from First Form to Seventh Form, or sixth grade to twelfth grade.

Girls and boys in each form had their own dormitory buildings. Kit was assigned to Rose Cottage, and while she attended Covington, she was supposed to earn points for her house by behaving and doing well in classes and school activities. Poor behavior and inferior achievements in classes and activities would lose house points. The more points a house earned, the better chance it had of winning the house trophy at the end of the year.

Kit liked the idea of such a competition. She had always been a good student, so she figured she'd ace a ton of points for Rose Cottage, win the trophy, and become amazingly popular. After all, why shouldn't she be popular? She was nice, she was honest, she worked hard, and even if she didn't ride, she could keep up with any of the other students in every other aspect just fine.

She was especially determined to show Elaine a thing or two.

She told Sally all about the stable fiasco as they toured the first floor of Rose Cottage, detailing Elaine's snobbish reaction. "She tried to kill me with her eyeballs," she insisted after Sally showed her the TV room.

"Hardly," Sally responded with a laugh, moving on to the little student kitchenette, with a cooker (not a stove), a tiny fridge ("No sneaking treats after bedtime," Sally warned), and the usual counters, cabinets, and sink. "You've just arrived," Sally continued as she led the way down the hall. "Elaine is just a tad . . . Well, you'll get to know each other better. Her room is just across from yours."

Kit stopped dead. "She lives here?"

Sally gestured her to keep moving. "She's the prefect for Rose Cottage."

They entered the common room, which looked like a little library with books on shelves, a couch, two desks, and a couple of chairs. "What's a prefect?" Kit asked while looking around.

"The student head of the residence."

"Oh, awesome," Kit grumbled. "Elaine can kill me with her eyeballs twenty-four hours a day."

"Or not." Sally led her next to what she referred to as the sunroom, a cute square room at the front of the cottage with lots of windows and a pane-glass roof. Kit had read that England didn't get that many warm, sunny days, so the idea of sunrooms made perfect sense.

Sally was still talking. "You know, I ended up making very good friends with the Elaine of my day at Covington."

"You went here?"

"Yes. Back in the Elizabethan era." Chuckling at her joke, Sally led Kit up the stairs and down another hall. She stopped before a closed door. "And here we are." She indicated for Kit to go inside.

Kit did. "Whoa!" she blurted out, totally overwhelmed. She forgot all about Elaine. This room, this gigantic space with two huge canopy beds and two desks and fancy wall sconces and a couch set and two armoires and a window seat—an actual window seat!—was going to be *her room*. "Wow!" She dropped her tote and overnight bag onto one of the stuffed chairs, struggling to control the urge to jump up and down.

Sally's big grin lit up her pretty face. "I'm just down the hall if you need me," she said, then left, closing the door behind her.

"Madhu, I have to go. My new roommate is here," a voice said softly.

Kit hadn't even noticed that she wasn't alone. Her new roommate sat on one of the canopy beds in front of an open laptop. "All warm wishes from your parents and me, Your Highness," said a voice from the laptop's speaker. Kit's roommate slammed the computer closed with an expression of dismay that vanished the second Kit noticed it.

Kit also noticed the girl's features. "Hey, I know you. From earlier, right?"

"Aren't you the one with the cowboy?" the girl responded.

Kit pointed to the laptop. "More importantly, did she just call you Your High—?"

"It's Anya." The girl thrust out her hand. "Nice to meet you."

"Kit." They shook hands. "Check out these beds. They're huge!" Kit's eyes took on a mischievous glint. "And fluffy." She couldn't hold it in anymore. She was so excited about everything, and here was the perfect release. It had to be done. There was just no choice in the matter.

She ran a couple of steps and launched herself face-first onto her bed with a satisfying *whump*. "Come on," she told Anya, laughing. "You know you want to."

Anya looked shocked. "Oh, I couldn't. It wouldn't be proper."

"Proper?" Kit asked, getting back to her feet. "Who cares? There's no one here."

Anya paused, thinking it over. She grinned as if contemplating doing the most unruly thing in all the universe—and then hopped onto her bed with hardly any energy at all. She giggled as if someone had tickled her. "You are correct! That was fun!"

Oh, dear. Kit realized that Anya might, in fact, be a bigger newbie than Kit herself. That tiny hop? It was pathetic. Clearly Anya needed coaching. "But you can do better," Kit urged her playfully.

"I can?"

"Oh, yeah. This time, really hurl yourself." Kit took a ready position. Anya copied her. "Ready? One, two, three!"

Both girls ran at their beds and flung themselves down, laughing.

The door opened. "What is going on here?" Sally demanded.

Kit and Anya answered at the same time: "Nothing, Miss Warrington!" competed with "Just playing on these wicked beds!"

Sally took a deep breath the way adults always did before delivering a lecture. "Now, I know you two are new to Covington, but surely you must know that such childish behavior is strictly forbidden." She zeroed in on Kit. "Katherine, I gave you some leeway earlier. However . . ." Sally let the sentence hang while Kit looked properly ashamed. Then, with a warning look at both girls, she exited.

Anya covered her face with her hands. "We can never do that again."

Kit couldn't believe it. How was Anya ever going to learn to have fun if she gave in so easily? "Oh, we *so* have to do that again!" she said.

Anya shook her head. "A rule is a rule."

"A rule is a guideline. At least that was my mom's take."

Anya made a point of sitting down on her bed properly. "Well, pink monkeys would tap-dance in the fountain before my parents would say that. I promised that if they allowed me to come to a real school, I wouldn't get into any trouble."

That caught Kit's radar. "What do you mean, a *real school*?"

Anya paused. "I've only had tutors. Homeschool."

"Dude, you gotta get out more."

In a more hopeful tone, Anya said, "Though I'm allowed to ride as much as I like as long as I keep my grades up. Shall we plan on a morning gallop together?"

Kit's mood balloon popped. Hadn't Nav invited her to do the same thing? It was true, then. *Everybody* at Covington rode except her. How was this possibly going to work?

She flopped back onto her bed face-first, but this time it wasn't much fun at all.

Kit's luggage arrived from the airport an hour later. Sally informed her that it would be brought to Rose Cottage along with several boxes of clothes and knickknacks that Kit had shipped to the school a week earlier. Kit found all of it stacked in the Rose Cottage entryway. With a groan, she hauled the first box up the stairs to her room and dumped it on the floor.

"I take it your belongings have arrived," Anya said. She was sitting at her desk reading some of the brochures from her Covington Welcome Packet. She gazed at Kit's box with curiosity. "May I ask what's in there?"

"Rocks, apparently," Kit complained, shaking out her strained arms. "Could have sworn I only packed clothes."

Anya giggled. "Come on, then. I'll help you carry the rest. I can't very well let my new roommate get arm cramps, now, can I?" The girls skipped down the stairs together. "Oh!" Anya said when she saw the pile of boxes and bags. "Is that . . . is that *it*?"

"That's it," said Kit. "My entire life, right here in this little pile. Kinda depressing, really."

"Of course it isn't," Anya said. "Having few belongings shows that you're not overly influenced by *things*, that you know who you are inside."

Kit laughed. "I wish." She hefted another box, noting from the corner of her eye how Anya tried to lift the third box but couldn't. Anya looked embarrassed, then quickly grabbed a couple of smaller bags instead. Kit grinned but said nothing.

The girls tramped up the stairs, down the hall, and into their room. Kit dumped her box on the floor while Anya carefully placed the bags on Kit's bed. "Can I help you unpack? I'd love to see what you brought."

Why is she so excited about something as dull as unpacking? Kit wondered. "It's just the usual stuff," she said. "You know, clothes, books, mementos—"

"Yes, but they're *your* clothes, books, and mementos. I'm curious." She added quickly, "I mean, about you, my new roommate!"

So the next hour was spent in a wave of chatter as the two new friends sorted through Kit's things and put every item neatly away. Just as Kit was beginning to wonder what was in *Anya's* closet, a dainty chime sounded over the room's speaker. "Attention, please,

Fourth-Form students. It is now time for tea," Sally's voice announced. "Please make your way to the dining hall to enjoy your first Covington meal together." The chime sounded once more as if to punctuate the announcement.

"Tea?" Kit asked in confusion. "Does she mean, like, high tea?" Kit wasn't sure what high tea even was, but she'd heard the term on TV.

"No, silly," Anya said. "Tea is the evening meal. Americans call it supper, right?"

"Oh!" Kit said. "Dinner! Yeah, let's go—I'm starved!"

When the girls arrived at the busy dining hall, Kit saw several familiar faces from earlier that day as the Fourth-Form students began lining up at one end of a long table loaded with plates and platters of food. "A buffet," Kit noted with approval. "Me like." She glanced behind her to get Anya's reaction only to discover that Anya wasn't there anymore.

She'd taken a seat at one of the tables.

Kit went over to her. "Earth to Anya, it's a buffet. The chow's over there." She pointed to the buffet line.

Anya shot to her feet. "Oh, right! I thought—I mean, I've never—"

"Oh, don't tell me," Kit said, and laughed. "Your mom always serves the food at dinner, doesn't she? My mom did that, too. Dad and I kept telling her she didn't have to. I mean, she wasn't a servant, you know? But she insisted on it, so we gave up and let her. Now, however, it's time for Kit and Anya 2.0, the Self-Serve Editions. Come on." Kit grasped Anya's arm and pulled her to the buffet line.

Kit grabbed a plate and peered into the first hot tray. "What's that?"

"Mmm, blood pudding!" said someone behind her.

"Oh. My. Gosh." Kit bent over to examine it more closely. The object in the tray looked like a giant worm, specifically a red wiggler, the kind that she and her dad used for bait when they went fishing back in Montana. This giant worm-thing was sliced up, and the inside had . . . spots. Of stuff. Unidentifiable spots of . . . worm-thing stuff. "I'm not eating that," she declared.

"But it's delicious," Anya said. "Do give it a try."

"I think I'll pass." Kit pointed at the bowl next to it. "What's the green goo?"

"Mushy peas. They're quite good, too."

"Mushy?" Kit asked. "What, they come pre-chewed?" *Maybe a buffet isn't so great after all,* she thought. Then she saw the plates of little hand-size pies and thought, *I like pie!* These pies weren't like any she had seen before, though. Labels on the plates identified them as steak and kidney pie, shepherd's pie, fish pie . . . "What is it with the English turning everything into pies?" she muttered, a little too loudly.

"Perhaps it's like you Americans' obsession with putting food on sticks," someone commented behind her.

Kit turned to see Nav, the handsome fellow who had gallantly saved her from being trampled by TK. He was beaming at her. She grinned back. "Touché."

His smile beamed even brighter.

Anya made a squeak of anxiety. "So many decisions. I don't know what to pick!" Her plate was still empty.

"Just go for it," Kit urged her. "You're free here. You can eat whatever you want. No parents, no pressure."

"But I need to eat a balanced meal."

"Oh, puh-lease." To give poor Anya inspiration, Kit heaped a pile of brussels sprouts (her favorite veggie, believe it or not) on her plate, then filled the rest of it with a mound of French fries, or *chips*, as the English called them (everybody knew that). "See this?" she said proudly of her choices. "Sprouts an' chips, a balanced meal. Sort of. Just pick something—you're holding up the line."

Anya's eyes lit up. "Are those samosas?" she asked, indicating a dish farther ahead.

"I believe so," Nav answered. "I can smell them. Heavenly."

With a rather guilty grin, Anya filled her plate with samosas. "Oh, and chips." She giggled, adding some of those, too. "My mother would faint to see me eating a combination like this!"

"Then mission accomplished," said Kit, not without relief. Anya really was holding up the line. They chose a table, sat down, and ate. And talked. And talked and ate. And Kit decided that she liked Anya very much.

When the desserts were brought out, Anya gasped. "They're serving sticky toffee pudding for afters!"

"Afters?" asked Kit with her mouth full of sprouts.

"Yes. After the meal."

"You mean dessert? Right. What did you call it again?"

"Sticky toffee pudding. Believe me, it's absolutely gorgeous."

As with so many things that day, Kit had never heard of it. But sticky was a good thing in a dessert. And toffee was definitely good, too. And she loved pudding. Therefore, sticky toffee pudding had to be yummy.

And it was. They each got a bowl of it and sat down again. "Mmm . . ." Anya groaned at her first mouthful.

"Mmm," Kit echoed in agreement. After she swallowed, she added, "Well, that does it. We're going to be good friends now for sure."

"Why do you say that?" asked Anya.

Kit shrugged. "If sticky toffee doesn't bond us together, nothing will."

Chapter 5

FITTING IN

It was time for the first day of class, and Kit was ready. She was beyond ready! She had gotten up early (she hadn't been able to sleep much the previous night anyway) and spent a half hour getting dressed, which was a very long time considering all she had to put on was a uniform.

The girls' standard uniform at Covington consisted of a white cotton button-up shirt, a gray skirt, dark-blue tights, a navy-blue blazer with red piping, black tasseled loafers, and of all things, a tie. A tie with stripes! The school patch on the blazer was kind of cool, but beyond that, the uniform was, well, way too uniformy.

So not my style, Kit thought when she got her first look at herself in the dorm room's big mirror. She felt like she was supposed to march onto a field during halftime. So, in typical Bridges fashion, she did something about it.

First off, the tights—or *stockings*, as they were called here—had to go. They made her look like she was going to ballet class. Instead, she put on her favorite cherry-red socks and replaced the black fringed loafers with her white leather Frye ankle boots for a little cowgirl flair. She took off the terrible tie and replaced it with a red bandana, added a thin red belt over the blazer, and as a finishing touch, put all her school supplies in her cross-body fringed leather boho purse. Perfect!

By the time she strode into her first class, she was feeling pretty and unique and confident. *This* was the way to start a new school year. She took a seat in front of Anya.

Her roomie eyed her "Kit Bridges style." "Wow," Anya said. "Your uniform looks amazing!" She quickly added, "I'd never risk it, but I love it."

Kit basked in the praise. It was about time she did something right around here. But in all honesty, she was more interested in the boy standing across the room, the fellow who had caught the runaway TK and who had been cornered by Elaine in the stable yesterday. "Who is that guy?" she asked.

Anya shrugged.

"Will Palmerston," piped up another student sitting in the next row. "He's been kicked out of Tonbridge, Charterhouse, *and* Harrow. Covington's kind of like his last chance before military school."

Kit never would have guessed that the tall, handsome stableboy was so troublesome, and she had never heard of those other schools. But they sounded impressive. "Wow, that's a big list," she said.

The student in the next row broke out in a huge smile. "You speak real English! Finally! It is so good to meet someone who kind of talks like me, you know?" He stuck his hand out. "I'm Josh Luders, from Alberta. Your dad's the stable master? That dude is so gnarly."

Kit shook Josh's hand, giving her dad a big check mark in her mental "Awesome" column.

That's when the class bell rang. Students scrambled to their desks seconds before Lady Covington entered the classroom.

Kit had expected to see a squat, white-haired, fuddy-duddy, old matron wearing a frumpy dress made out of couch fabric or something, but Lady Covington was nothing like that. Tall, dressed in a smart brown skirt suit, her soft ginger hair swept up in a neat French twist, she instantly commanded the classroom by simply standing there. "Settle down," she said. "I'm not here to whisk anyone off to the dungeon."

Kit relaxed. At least the headmistress had a sense of humor.

Lady Covington strolled down the first aisle of desks. "As you know," she said, "we expect excellence at Covington. It is my goal to be named U.K. Boarding School of the Year. Therefore, it is *your* goal as well." Her eyes landed on Will Palmerston, who, Kit noticed, looked immediately guilty. "There will be zero tolerance for pranks and the like. Any such behavior will result in the execution . . ."

Kit tensed. *No way!* she thought.

"Of appropriate detentions and/or expulsions. Are we clear?"

Whew.

Lady Covington walked back to the front of the class. "Yes?" she said when Elaine raised her hand.

"Lady Covington, has there been a change to the uniform? I've noticed some infractions." Elaine glanced over her shoulder at Kit.

The headmistress also looked at Kit. "Katherine Bridges. Please stand."

"Hey, that's me!" Kit said, popping to her feet. "How did you know my—?"

"Could you explain to me what on earth you are wearing?"

Kit automatically corrected her. "It's Kit. I go by Kit."

"A kit is a travel bag or a small fox, not a young lady, *Katherine*." The headmistress spoke with such perfect diction and authority that Kit felt like she'd just been insulted by a Shakespearean actor.

"Okay," Kit said. "Uh, I was inspired to make the uniform my own, to express my individuality." Surely Lady Covington could understand that.

"Any alteration to the Covington uniform is strictly prohibited."

Fine, then here's my chance, Kit thought. *I'll show everybody how levelheaded and rational I can be. That'll be good.* "But maybe we could have a discussion about it," she suggested with a big smile. "What do you think, Lady C?"

"We have already had the discussion," Lady Covington replied. Her voice took on a dark tone. "And my name is *Lady Covington*."

Mistake! Backfire! Retreat! Kit thought, trying to keep her smile going. She didn't dare say another word out loud, and her smile wilted as every student stared at her.

Lady Covington nodded to the rest of the class. "Good day," she said, dismissing the entire interaction, and she strode out of the room.

Dead silence was broken by Josh. "Dude," he said to Kit, "you just stood up to Lady C on the first day. Very bold move."

Kit figured that "bold" really meant "stupid." She noticed Will grinning in a sort of pained way, while Elaine appeared quite pleased with how things had gone.

Kit wondered if she was ever going to do anything right again.

Chapter 6

RULES & REGULATIONS

L ater that day, Kit found her dad out by the practice ring teaching his first riding class.

He wasn't actually teaching. Before he could make any firm teaching plans, he needed to see what the students could already do. So he was running them through a short jumper course.

Kit hadn't yet seen the academy's official riding uniform, and she was surprised how smart and professional it made the students look. The weather was cold, so everyone had donned their warm navy-blue jackets with bright-red side panels and, of course, the Covington crest patch on the front (Kit presumed they were wearing their regular uniform riding coats underneath). Cream-colored breeches, tall black riding boots, and a black helmet finished the look.

Even the horses were in uniform, all of them wearing matching protective boots. It was all very stylish.

Covington stylish, anyway, Kit thought. She preferred her dad's cowboy apparel for riding, but even he wasn't dressed like a proper cowboy anymore. Hugging her own jacket closer against the breeze, she reached his side and leaned on the rail to watch the next rider.

It was Elaine. She guided her horse up and over the first jump, the second jump, and the third jump. Kit marveled at how smoothly the horse moved, with its ears flicking back and forth, showing that the animal was relaxed and listening to its rider's signals. Not a single rail fell. "Good one, Elaine," Rudy called to her when she finished the course. "Nice work!"

Elaine nodded at the compliment as if it were a foregone conclusion.

Kit rolled her eyes and turned to her dad. "Nice tie," she snarked playfully.

He gave a soft growl, the sound he always made when he was annoyed. "Lady C made me wear it." He tugged at the ascotlike material bunched up under his red work-shirt collar. "I'm gonna suffocate in this thing."

"If the cowboys could see you now," Kit teased him again, pulling her cell phone — or *mobile*, as it was called in England — out of her pocket.

Rudy saw the move. "Don't you even think about —"

Before he could finish, Kit raised the phone, and it gave a little *click*. "Ha!" She laughed, checking her handiwork. The photo was perfect, with Kit smiling and Rudy frowning in his cute, grumpy way. She hit the Send button. "Too late!" she announced as the e-mail zipped away through the ether to the other side of the world, where her father's cowboy friends would be sure to laugh their chaps off when they saw it.

Rudy sighed.

At least Lady Covington was letting him wear his Stetson, Kit thought. Once a cowboy, always a cowboy.

As Nav rode his horse into the starting position, Rudy said, "Now, Kit, watch these guys ride." His voice took on a thoughtful tone. "Could be you."

Kit watched as Nav seemed to float his horse effortlessly from jump to jump. He rode a good course and gave Kit a suave wave as he returned to the group of students by the rails.

Next came Anya, who rode gracefully, as if she weren't sitting on her horse but was actually part of it. Another good course.

Then came Josh. Kit noticed that he didn't display so much a smooth riding style as an athletic one, with a cocky confidence that made Kit grin. Up and over, up and over he rode, but at the last jump, his horse's rear right hoof knocked against a rail, sending it tumbling. He gave Kit a cheeky smile as he passed by anyway, as if he'd intended to knock that rail down.

Last came Will. Everybody stopped what they were doing to watch him, and Kit quickly saw why. He spurred his horse to a faster pace than the others, approaching each jump as if it might run away before he could reach it. His horse's longer strides meant that it could make fewer strides between jumps, but Will had obviously walked the course beforehand, calculating how many strides his mount would need to make at such speed without ending up too close or too far from each jump to clear it comfortably.

"Go easy, Will! Don't push it!" Rudy called to him. Despite his speed, Will rode a good course.

As the students debated the technical merits and faults of their rounds, Rudy turned to his daughter.

"I heard that you gave Lady Covington some of that infamous Kit Bridges lip in class this morning."

"I barely said anything!" Kit responded. "This place is practically built out of rules, and I don't know any of them."

"Well, you better rein in that attitude, and fast. I don't want to hear about you talking back again."

Kit saluted. "Okay, I hear you." The salute was meant as a joke, but she knew that her father's warning was serious.

Rudy nodded. The school bell rang, and he called out to his students, "All right, good work today. We'll talk technique next class." He headed back to the stables.

Kit walked over to the knot of students and horses. She arrived in time to hear Elaine tell Anya, "Your counter-canter was way off, Patel. You can't just go and add your own little twist to it like that."

"But that's the way I was taught it," Anya said.

"Well, it's not the *right* way. You'd lose points, which would cost us. Everyone has to be perfect. *You* have to be perfect."

Kit didn't like the way Anya slumped in her saddle at Elaine's criticism, so she blurted out, "You killed that course, Elaine," hoping that praise would soothe the girl's ego and make her back off. "You looked good, too, Anya," she added hastily. "And what's wrong with her doing it the way she wants to do it?"

"What's *wrong*," Elaine snapped, "is that it isn't *right*."

"Well, I thought it looked awesome."

Kit had already noticed Elaine's ability to make anyone she glared at feel about two inches tall. Elaine now turned that glare on Kit. "How could *you* possibly understand?"

Yup. Kit could practically feel herself shrinking. She turned around and scurried to the stables.

She found her dad in the tack room, lunching on a grilled cheese sandwich. He handed her a plate with another sandwich on it. Kit gave him a hug then accepted the plate and sat down. She took a huge bite and moaned, "This is so good, Dad." She chewed and swallowed. "It almost makes me forget about all the horse stuff."

"Tastes like home, doesn't it?"

"Yeah." Kit examined the grilled cheese yummi-ness in her hand. "They only use one piece of bread here, and they call it *cheese on toast*. It's just so wrong." She took another bite and added with a full mouth, "But this is delicious!"

Rudy eyed her carefully. Kit knew he could sense that something was up and was just waiting to hear the details. She glanced away and then at him again.

"I gotta tell you something," she finally said.

Rudy waited, chewing.

"I don't think it's going to work out between me and Covington. Aside from the fact that I have to wear a prison uniform all day, I don't ride."

Rudy took a breath as if to speak.

"And I know what you're going to say: Why not give it a try? Well—"

"Actually, what I was going to say was what you said to me when we first got here. Change is good, even if it takes some getting used to. Remember what your mom used to always say? 'Whatever you do, do it with all your might . . .'"

Kit finished, "'Things done by halves are never done right.'"

"That's the spirit, Kit."

Kit thought about it. "So I just keep going?"

Rudy sighed. "Yeah."

Even though he'd just given her a pep talk, Kit recognized the sadness that had crept into his voice. She moved closer to him on the bench and laid her head on his shoulder. "I miss her, too, Dad," she said softly. She thought that he might say something more, but her dad had never been the kind to talk about emotional stuff, especially if the emotions happened to be his own.

He pulled away from her, kindly but pointedly. "I have to get ready for my next class." He started fiddling with the papers on his desk.

"Dad?" Kit asked after a moment.

"Yeah?"

"What if I'm . . . scared?"

"Well, you used to be scared of ghosts and brussels sprouts." He tousled her hair the way he used to when she was a kid. She hated it and made a face, but deep inside her, something cold warmed up a little. She missed her mother so much, and she knew how hard her dad was fighting to stay positive. He had loved her mother with all his heart, and watching him struggle day after day without her by his side often made Kit cry.

But she couldn't afford to cry anymore. Her dad needed her to do well at Covington, so she would do her best, no matter the circumstances. And she would begin by wrapping up the rest of her grilled-cheese for later.

That was the plan, anyway. No sooner had she picked up a plastic bag to put it in than she heard a nearby horse snuffle. TK was standing in the doorway, which meant that he'd escaped his stall again. "TK? What the—"

He peeked in at her, but something seemed to disturb him. His ears flicked back and his nostrils flared as he backed up the way he'd come, disappearing from sight.

"Hey, what do you think you're doing?" Kit hurried out and found him standing near the stable doorway, ears twitching. "What are you doing out of your stall? What is it? What—"

TK bolted outside.

"No, no, no, no, no!" Kit cried, following him. He was so doggone jittery! What was causing it? "Easy, take it easy," she told him. He'd stopped in front of the main school building, so she cautiously approached. "What is your problem?" She kept her voice soft and held her arms out to show him there was nothing to be afraid of.

TK tossed his head with another tense grunt.

Kit looked where his nose kept pointing, at her hand — her hand that was still holding the plastic bag. "It's just a bag."

TK pawed the dirt, ears flicking back and forth. His tail swished. It almost looked like he was telling her to take the bag away.

Kit stuffed it into her pocket, out of sight. "Look," she said, holding out her empty hands for him to see.

The nervous glint in TK's eyes disappeared. His ears swung forward, and he lowered his head. Was he actually apologizing?

"I'm not mad," Kit assured him, "even though it is your fault that I'm on Elaine's hit list."

At that, TK snorted.

"Oh, really? Then you try being the new girl."

TK nickered.

"You know what? I don't blame you for busting out." Kit touched his muzzle. He let out a hot horse-breath sigh as if he liked her touch, so she began to pet him.

What Kit didn't know was that she was being watched. From the student lounge in the main building, Will, Anya, Josh, Nav, and Elaine were observing the scene. "Spectacular," Nav said in wonder. "That girl is full of surprises."

And from her office window up on the second floor, Lady Covington was also watching, her expression one of intense interest.

Outside, Kit wondered what might be TK's real problem. Why did he always try to escape? *I don't like rules,* she thought. *What if he doesn't, either?* She decided to remove his bridle. "You know," she said as she unbuckled the cheek piece, "if I could chew through my rope and wind up back home, I might do it. This place has too many rules." She lifted the halter over his ears and slid it off his head. The bridle was off. "You good?"

TK grunted, tossing his head as if pleased with his new freedom.

Kit laughed. "You're welcome! All you had to do was ask. Why is everyone so afraid of you, anyway?

You're not scary—as long as I don't have to actually *ride* you. I don't like the tie, and you don't like the lead."

When TK nodded his big head and whinnied, Kit's eyes grew wide. "Were you just saying yes? When you nod your head like that?"

TK nodded again, then shook his head happily, making his long forelock and mane flop one way then the other.

Kit couldn't believe it. "I'm talking to a horse! That's so cool!"

In the main building's lounge, five students continued to watch the scene. "Whoa, that's a gift," Josh said. "Will, even you couldn't get him to do that."

"I know," Will agreed.

Anya just stared out the window in amazement. "That *is* a gift."

Only Elaine remained unimpressed. "Would you guys stop drooling over her? That horse is a weirdo and so is she. They're perfect for each other."

Outside, Kit was growing bolder. She backed up, then motioned with her hand. "TK, come."

TK walked to her.

Gleefully giggling, Kit improvised a goofy little dance, sidestepping and bouncing on her toes. "Know what a dance is?" she challenged him.

TK seemed to drink up her happy energy and rocked back and forth, prancing in place. Kit kept hopping and sidestepping, and TK hopped along with her, shaking his head and snorting.

As he did, another secret spectator pushed his Stetson back from his forehead and stared in wonder at his daughter and the dancing horse.

Chapter 7

THROWING DOWN THE GAUNTLET

School days at Covington started with homeroom, known as registration or tutor time, when teachers took roll call and made general announcements. When Kit made her entrance to registration the next morning, she was glad to see that Lady Covington was already in the classroom, as was Sally. Most of the other students were in their seats, too. *Good,* she thought. Everything was in place for her to make her own big announcement.

It was all TK's fault. He'd given her the idea the day before when they were dancing. During that moment, for the first time since arriving at Covington, Kit had felt free. She had felt like herself, not a confused newbie or a nonriding outsider, but Kit Bridges, daughter of Rudy and Elizabeth Bridges of Montana, U.S.A. It had been wonderful. So she had come up with an idea to keep that feeling.

It was either that or go completely bananas.

"Miss Bridges," came the headmistress's voice before Kit even reached her seat. Kit obediently turned around as the head of the school scrutinized her from head to foot. "Are you aiming for a detention?" Lady Covington demanded.

Kit had her speech ready. "Good morning, Lady Covington. According to the Covington Book of Rules and Regulations, I *am* wearing my uniform to code."

"That is, however, a *boys'* uniform—from the turn of last century!"

That was entirely true. Kit had gotten her hands on a pair of gray pinstriped trousers, a black knit vest, and even a pocket watch, the chain of which hung in a proper loop from her vest pocket. Last, she had fashioned a bow tie in the proper school colors by cutting up her regular tie. She wore her usual white uniform shirt, shoes, and blazer. She thought she looked pretty spiffy, considering.

But that wasn't the point. They hadn't gotten to the point yet. "Who's to say, really, if this is a boys' or girls' uniform?" Kit asked.

Lady Covington's eyes flared. "*I'm* to say."

Kit almost withered under that look, but she fought to maintain her courage, knowing that she was in deep now. She *had* to make her point. All the other students were watching in awe. "Fair enough," she said. "Would you also say that all your students are great riders?"

The shift in topic came suddenly, but Lady Covington obviously knew the arts of discussion and debate. With a hint of curiosity in her tone, she smoothly replied, "Well, I would certainly say that they're on their way to getting there."

"Even though they all ride differently?"

Now Lady Covington was getting miffed. "Your point?"

"I respect that you have your own way of doing things around here, but"—Kit gestured at her roommate—"look at Anya. She rides so gracefully, she's like a bird or something. Put that with Will's raw talent and Josh's determination, and you've got a serious secret weapon." Anya, Will, and Josh grinned in surprise while Lady Covington remained silent, so Kit went on. "Nav sails over jumps like they're nothing, and Elaine is technically and strategically perfect." Nav's face lit up with one of his trademark suave smiles, while Elaine didn't move a muscle. Kit ran for the finish line: "Mash up those skills, and you've got something deadly. We're all different, and that's okay. And that's why I'm wearing this outfit, because . . . I need to be me."

Kit waited, wondering if the world—her world—was about to crash down upon her forever. She expected Lady Covington to make some kind of response, but of all people, it was Anya who spoke next. "I need to be me, too," she said, and stood up, looping a red scarf around her neck.

Nav stood up and removed his blazer. "This is a little more me," he said, still smiling.

At the front of the class, Sally stood still as a stone, her eyes big and round, her eyebrows crawling up her forehead as she regarded her boss. Nobody knew what was going to happen next.

Lady Covington seemed to be holding a formal debate in her own head, herself versus herself. Several expressions grabbed at her features so that it was impossible to tell precisely what she was thinking. She finally let out an infuriated, "Oh!" and stormed for the door. Kit thought she was going to leave, but the woman stopped in the doorway and whirled around to face the class. "Very well," she stated in a crisp voice. "No detention."

Kit was sure that the entire class screamed a silent *what?*

"There will, however, be a new Covington rule book. Posthaste." She strode out.

The tension in the air popped, with everybody giggling, laughing, and gasping in stunned relief. Sally released the breath she'd been holding in a big *whoof* sound, giving Kit what Rudy referred to as the *you're lucky to be alive* look. Anya patted Kit's shoulder, and Josh gave Kit a high five. Even Will, who was usually so reserved, grinned at Kit in amazement.

But not everything was grins and cheering. When Kit went to the stables later on, Elaine intercepted her. "Lady Covington never bends the rules for anybody," she stated flatly.

"She didn't really bend anything," Kit said. "I got her on a technicality."

"Still." Elaine frowned. "She never gives up that easy. Something's not right."

Kit was tempted to respond, but she decided it wasn't worth it. Besides, she felt good. She had made her point. That's all she'd wanted to do. She headed for TK's stall, pulling a fat carrot out of her pocket. It was only right that TK should share in the celebration, after all.

But the stall was empty. "TK?" she called. "You'd better not be pulling another disappearing act on me. We have to take this show on the road!"

There was no response, so Kit headed out into the back courtyard. There she found TK being led toward a horse trailer by a stranger. Her father was there, too. "Dad, what is going on? What is this?"

"Lady C ordered that he be shipped out," replied Rudy as TK began giving his handler a rough time. He reared up and whinnied.

"Shipped out to where?" Kit asked.

Rudy spoke reluctantly. "Auction. I'm sorry, Kit. It's her call. I saw you earlier. . . . I know this must be hard, but nobody rides him. And you've seen how he behaves."

"But I can change that! She can't do this! I won't let her! Dad, we can't!"

As if in agreement, TK reared up again, forcing his handler to back away as lethal hooves pawed the air.

Ignoring the danger, Kit stepped over to him, hand held out. TK quieted the moment she touched him. "It's okay, boy," she said, stroking his neck as he nuzzled her. How could this be happening? Everything had looked so sunny, and now it was all going wrong! She knew that her dad would fix the situation if he could, but still she pleaded, "Dad, this is the first time in years that I haven't been afraid of a horse!"

Rudy grimaced, hating his words even as he said them. "Honey, back up. You're making a scene."

"I don't care! I have to do something!"

"There's nothing we can do," Rudy said, the pain in his face clear.

"Well, I have to do something!" Kit marched to the base of the trailer ramp and sat down in front of it. "I am not moving until TK is back in his stall. Tell Lady C if you have to, but I am not moving." Then she folded her arms and lay down on the ground, in the straw and mud, not caring one whit. TK was worth it. He was so worth it!

All she needed was for Lady Covington to understand that.

Chapter 8

DRAWING A LINE
IN THE MUD

That evening, the scene outside Lady Covington's office was not entirely normal. Three uniformed students stood with their ears pressed against the closed door.

"We're going to get into trouble!" Anya whispered.

Nav nodded. "This is breaking at least four rules."

"Go, then," Will hissed in irritation. "I mean, if you're *scared*."

That got Nav right where it hurt. "No," he whispered quickly. "I'm good."

"I can't believe Kit just lay right down in the mud!" Anya whispered. "Oh, it must be so shouty in there. . . ."

"With Lady Covington?" Nav shuddered. "Shouting isn't imposing enough. She *whispers*, like she's shooting icicles straight into your soul."

Will moved closer to the door. "Shhh."

Inside the office, Kit stood before Lady Covington's desk, her boy's uniform caked with mud. Mud was on her hands, in her hair—everywhere.

Seated at her desk, Lady Covington was speaking angrily about that very fact. "And we do not lie in the mud at Covington!"

"It was a protest!" Kit explained. "I didn't want you to take my horse away!"

"That animal is going to auction whether you lay in the mud or not."

"But I—"

"An unruly horse in the stable is both a hindrance and dangerous, to say nothing of the fact that no one is riding him."

"Then *I'll* ride him!" Kit blurted out.

Lady Covington almost did a double take. "You're terrified of horses, and yet you cannot live without the wildest horse in the stable. And now you're saying you'll ride him. Why?"

"I don't think he's wild," Kit said, groping to make sense of what she herself had only recently discovered. "I just think he's misunderstood. Please, give us a chance."

"He's had chances, plenty of them."

"But not with me!"

Lady Covington sighed.

Outside the door, Sally discovered three students in a place where they weren't supposed to be. "Hello, all," she greeted them cheerfully. "Waiting to see the headmistress?"

Nav, Anya, and Will spun around. They couldn't have looked more guilty if they'd tried. "I—I—I was merely passing by. I'm late for tea. Good-bye!" Anya said, and darted away.

That left Nav and Will. "Boys," Sally said firmly, "this behavior is strictly—"

They were gone before she could finish, which was fine with Sally. They knew she wouldn't forget this incident anytime soon. After shaking her head in dismay at their unruliness, she paused, waiting until they were completely out of sight. Then she pressed her own ear to the door.

Inside, Lady Covington said, "I will create a schedule that you will follow." She pulled open one of her desk drawers and hauled out a big, thick intimidating book. "This is the Covington Training Manual. Commit it to memory. Eat, sleep, and breathe it. Your training will commence tomorrow." She thunked it down on her desk.

Kit was in shock. "Did . . . did I just say I would ride a horse?"

"Yes, you did. And if you're going to compete in the midterm event, you had better get started."

Kit took the book, which weighed about a ton, and exited the office, thinking, *What just happened?*

At breakfast the next morning, Anya sat next to Kit. "Okay," she said, setting down a bowl of fruit and a glass of orange juice, "you have to tell me everything."

Kit fiddled with the spoon in her oatmeal. "Well, I panicked and sort of promised that I would—"

"I know. We weren't just eavesdropping. We were there for backup."

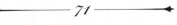

"Invisible backup?"

"That's the only kind we could muster," Anya admitted. "I'm sorry."

"That's okay. I get it." Kit glanced over at the big red banner hanging over the teachers' table in the dining room. It read:

COVINGTON WELCOMES
BINGHAM ACADEMY
RIDE WITH PRIDE

"So what's the deal with this opening race?" Kit asked. "It's all anybody can talk about."

"Actually, it's called *eventing*," said Anya, but she didn't explain what it meant. She was more focused on the other part of the opening event festivities. "I'm super excited about the gala. What are we going to wear?"

Kit didn't know what a gala was any more than she knew what *eventing* meant. "There's a dress code?"

"Kit," Anya said in disbelief, "it's a *gala*! I have so much to do! I have to choose the right gown, select the appropriate accessories—"

Kit was lost. "Gown?"

Josh took a seat next to Anya, setting down a plate stacked with pancakes along with a set of silverware and a linen napkin. "I can't decide between my tweed suit and my tuxedo and top hat," he declared in a worried tone.

"A tweed suit is considered day wear," Anya advised him.

Kit laughed. "He's teasing you."

Anya gave him a stern look, and Josh shrugged. "It's what I do. What are you stressed about, anyway? You must have people to do all of that stuff for you. Dresses and all that."

Kit figured he was teasing Anya again, but like a turtle, Anya ducked her head down closer to her shoulders as if trying to hide. "Whatever could you mean?" she asked nervously. "I don't have *people*. I'm going to handle this all by myself. Just me."

"My first tip?" Josh said. "No gowns. It's a disco."

"A what?" As far as Kit had ever heard, discos were those cheesy places in the '70s where guys wore dorky polyester suits and danced by pointing their fingers around like John Travolta.

"That's what they call a dance here," Josh informed her.

"Oh," said Kit. "Good to know. I was going to have to ask my dad for some old-school dance moves."

All conversation in the dining hall stopped as Elaine entered. "Ladies and gentlemen," she said in her best *I'm making an announcement so shut it* voice, "the opening event is upon us. The season starts the second our enemies step onto our turf. We need to bring our top game." She sounded so serious and intense that Kit threw an amused look to Anya, who tried to suppress her own smirk. Elaine noticed the exchange. "This isn't funny," she snapped at them. "Bingham Academy is coming. This is a BSEA event. Everything counts."

Josh noticed Kit's confusion and explained, "BSEA. British Schools Equestrian Association. It's the league we compete in."

Elaine passed out papers that showed photos of each Bingham competitor and their team stats. "Everything you need to know about Beatrice Bates is on this sheet," she said gravely.

"And that is her nemesis," Josh continued softly, making Kit grin. *So Elaine has a nemesis, huh?* she thought. *Don't superheroes have those—mortal enemies they have to battle every time they turn around?*

This was indeed crucial information.

Elaine suddenly realized what she'd said and swiftly corrected herself. "I mean, everything you need to know about *Bingham Academy* is on this sheet," she said. "They are our number-one competitors. Memorize it: their weaknesses, their strengths, their rank, even what they eat for breakfast. Write 'Defeat Bates' on top of your schedules." She was so wound up that she didn't realize she'd mentioned her nemesis again.

Anya turned to Kit. "Do you have a copy of our schedule?"

"It's on your phone," Kit replied. "They sent it by e-mail."

"Oh. I seem to have deleted my e-mail . . . and lost my phone."

Kit started to laugh at her roomie but stopped short when Lady Covington stepped up to the teachers' table. "Your attention, please! Following years of tradition, Covington will ride to victory on Saturday. If we are going to rank first place, we must show our opponents exactly who we are. And to be clear: we are winners. This is a significant stone on our path to being named U.K. Boarding School of the Year." She paused to let that last point sink in. "Thank you."

As she stepped down, Elaine's cell phone beeped. She gaped at it in horror. "Oh, no, no, no, no, no, no!"

She was standing near Josh, so he pulled her hand down so that he could see what was on the phone's screen. Kit and Anya caught a glimpse, too—a photo of Elaine at about eight years old. One of her front teeth was missing, leaving a goofy gap in her smile, and her bangs (or *fringe*) had been cut way too high and crooked, to boot. There was a message printed under it: "Elaine W. is my toughest competition this weekend? I've cleared my trophy cabinet."

Elaine shook with rage. "Beatrice Bates, you will pay for this!"

Chapter 9

COMPETITION COMPLICATIONS

Kit almost felt sorry for Elaine.

Almost.

The photo made the rounds at lightning speed. As Kit later walked to her dad's office in the stable, she passed clumps of students giggling and whispering about it. Normally Kit would have joined in the fun, but she had more important things to worry about.

"Oh, good," she said when she found Rudy about to start teaching. "Dad, this is huge. I can't get TK out of his stall, and I need to get to work with him ASAP—"

"I heard." Rudy regarded his daughter with deep pride and just a little bit of amusement. "Welcome to your first riding class."

Kit wasn't signed up for a riding class. *I guess I am now*, she thought.

Elaine strode into the room, buzzing with anxiety. "When do we tack up?" she practically demanded of Rudy. "This is meant to be a riding lesson. I need to annihilate Beatrice Bates. I trained all summer!"

The knot of boys waiting for class snickered. "Is that before or after you grew some front teeth?" Will taunted, holding up his phone.

"And got rid of that unfortunate yellow fringe!" Nav snickered.

"That was a dare!" Elaine exploded. "I grabbed the wrong scissors!" She continued more softly, "Bates won't know what hit her, which will be my trophy. In the back of her head." When the boys stopped laughing and eyed her warily, she clarified in a prim voice, "By accident, of course."

Rudy cleared his throat. "Intuition. It's the foundation of all riding. Today, each of you is going to spend some time with your horse. Hang out with them. Talk to them. Really listen."

Elaine didn't like that idea one bit. "Sir, respectfully, we don't have time for this. We need to prepare."

Rudy acknowledged her statement with a nod, then continued, "A deep connection with your horse is the most important aspect of riding." When Elaine tried to interrupt again, he leaned down so that he was eye to eye with her. "You can't connect with rules."

"I need to connect with winning," Elaine declared boldly.

Kit was amazed when her father ignored the comment. "Grab your stools and head out into the stable," he instructed everyone. When Elaine refused to budge, he clapped his hands as if to shoo away pesky squirrels. "No time like the present to start that horse-human bond!"

He made Elaine back down by taking charge, Kit thought, impressed. *And he did it not just with words but with actions—just like when you train a horse.* Maybe she needed to do the same. She stepped in front of her dad and stated firmly, "Well, I've got the whole horse bonding thing covered, so can I just skip right to riding?"

Rudy laid his hand on her shoulder and guided her out the door. "I'm loving your enthusiasm, kiddo, but first things first, eh?"

So much for that.

Later, in Rose Cottage, Anya sat on her wonderfully fluffy bed with her laptop open. "Madhu, that's way too fancy," she told the laptop.

"You said it was a gala," the laptop replied reasonably.

"Yes, well, galas are a little bit different over here."

On the laptop screen, a lovely Indian woman — Madhu — held several dresses in one hand. With the other, she held up a particularly beautiful purple dress studded with sparkling gems.

Anya's eyes went wide. "Wow — *no*. I can't. I'll totally stand out!"

"Which you were born to do, Your Highness," Madhu replied.

"Not here. Here I want to be like the others. That's why I haven't told anybody."

"That you are a pr —?"

"Shhhh!" Anya hissed, looking around to make sure nobody was listening, which was silly because she was alone in her bedroom.

Madhu spoke again. "There is no shame in this."

Anya knew that. She'd had this discussion with Madhu and her parents many times. They just didn't understand. "I'm not ashamed," she told Madhu for probably the hundredth time. "I just want to be like the others for once. And I can't do that if people are still treating me like a princess."

"As you wish," Madhu said. "You know where I am if you need me."

Anya performed a quick *namaste* gesture to her governess and closed her laptop with a sigh. "Okay," she told herself, "I can do this."

Meanwhile, Kit was on her way to the mini tuckshop in the main school building to get a chocolate bar. She had successfully ducked out of her dad's class, but now she didn't know what to do. Eating chocolate seemed logical, so chocolate it was—until Lady Covington turned a corner and spied her.

"Katherine, what are you doing in here? I thought you would be spending every spare moment on that horse."

Kit tried not to squirm. "Uh, he's not feeling it today," she said.

That didn't go over well with the headmistress. "*He* is not in charge. You will tack him up, and control him while riding in the ring before we enter into any other discussions. Do it now."

Great. Kit was fully aware that she had promised to ride TK. She even *wanted* to ride him. Kind of. In a ride-him-but-not-really-ride-him sort of way. That, of course, wasn't going to work any better than ditching her dad's class was working, so she just stood there, her stomach churning along with her anxiety. "I—" she began, having no idea what she was going to say. As it turned out, no words came to mind.

"Close your mouth, Katherine. You are going to catch flies."

Kit snapped her mouth shut.

"Now, if you will excuse me, I must prepare for my annual unavoidable luncheon with the headmistress of Bingham Academy."

Despite the circumstances, Kit couldn't resist this tidbit of information. Was there some kind of problem between the headmistresses? *Juicy*, she thought, and fished for more. "Not a fan of Lady Branson?"

"*Headmistress* Branson," Lady Covington stated, "is no lady."

"Burn!"

"Enough with the editorials, Katherine. You have work to do." Lady Covington jabbed a finger in the general direction of the stables.

Kit started walking.

In the stables, Rudy's students were taking time to bond with their mounts as per their teacher's instructions. Will's and Nav's horses were in stalls next to each other, so the two boys talked while they groomed.

"Have you used a double bridle?" Nav asked.

"No," Will replied. "Doubles only belong on horses with hard mouths."

"What makes you say that?"

Will gave his bay gelding a pat on the neck. "Wayne here told me. We're best mates now." He always referred to his horse as Wayne, thought the bay gelding's full name was Sir Gawain in honor of the famous knight in the King Arthur legends.

Nav chuckled. "I'm using a double. But it's not because Prince has a hard mouth. I just prefer it." At the sound of his name, Prince gave a snort. Nav scratched him around the ears.

"Good thing you don't need my permission, then."

The two students continued their vigorous brushing for a moment. Then Nav said, "Are you asking anyone to the gala?"

"Are you asking me or your horse?" Will quipped. "I'm off girls," he answered seriously.

"Ah. Wise. From what I hear, you can't afford any more trouble in your life."

Will snorted much like Prince had done earlier. "Thanks for the thoughtful reminder."

Nav spoke again, almost nervously. "I was planning on asking someone . . . to the Gala."

Kit bounced into the stable. "Hey, guys," she greeted them.

Nav smiled at her, his perfect teeth gleaming. "We were just talking about you."

That made Will turn around. Kit took advantage and asked them both, "Which one do you like better?" She held up the two saddle pads she was carrying, one red, one blue. "I'm thinking of getting TK all gussied up for some dressige."

The boys exchanged grins. "Dressige!" Nav chuckled. "I think you mean dressaaaage," and he lingered on the "a" to make the point about pronunciation.

Will explained, "It's a type of riding. You know, rider and horse run a test where every movement is judged."

"Oh." Kit hunched her shoulders sheepishly. "I thought it was some kind of fancy horse dress-up. My bad. Lady C is just demanding to see my *equestrian arts*." She shrugged. "I'll figure it out."

"I can help!"

Kit paused. Was she hearing double? Both boys had spoken the exact same words at the exact same time. With a knowing smirk, she watched their formerly mutual amusement turn into mutual suspicion. They both liked her!

Wicked, she thought.

In less than ten minutes, she had both boys showing her how to tack up TK. She had grown up around horses and had ridden until she was eight, true, but mostly her dad had tacked up for her and she'd ridden Western, so she had no idea how to put on TK's English tack. First came the saddle. "Then, your right arm, holding the bridle, goes up over his ears."

Kit started to do as Nav instructed, but Will, who stood by TK's flank stroking him and, in general, keeping him calm, argued, "No, he's head shy. She could end up with twenty kilos of horse skull bashing her in the nose."

Nav ignored the advice. "Remain calm," he told Kit, "and the horse will know who is in charge." Nav helped as Kit got the bit into TK's mouth. She gently pulled the headstall over his ears, then buckled the nosebend and throatlatch. Done! She was pleased with her success and barely heard Nav say, "So I was thinking about the gala—"

TK snorted, shaking his head in irritation.

"Oh, no," said Kit. "He's getting that look, his freak-out face."

"Well, right," Will said in a *duh* tone. "That's because he needs different handling. Saying *remain calm* is not going to cut it." He aimed that last comment at Nav.

Nav, however, was lost in his own world. "I wondered if you might consider going to the—"

TK bolted.

"Again? Seriously?" Will grumbled, running after the horse.

Nav actually seemed pleased with what was happening. While Kit flapped her hands helplessly and TK cantered farther and farther away, he pressed her for an answer. "Was that a yes?"

Kit started running after Will. "Whatever—just help us get TK!"

As Will and Kit ran after TK, Nav punched the air. "Yes! Well done, Navarro. Seems like you've won yourself a date!"

In the student lounge, Elaine sat alone at a study desk fuming about the riding class she had just finished—the *pointless* riding class, in her opinion. Bonding with a horse? Really! Good riders mastered their horses, period, and they did this by riding them correctly again and again and again and again and however many times it took to teach the horse to do things *right*. The upcoming opening event wasn't going to be won by *bonding*, no matter what Rudy Bridges said.

Enough was enough. She opened her laptop, went to the search engine, and typed in "Rudy Bridges." What kind of credentials did he have, anyway, that made him an acceptable riding instructor to Lady Covington? Was the school going soft?

She hit the Search button and studied the results. The first headline read, "Rudy Bridges: Jumpers, Hunters, Equitation, Dressage, Eventing." The article began, "As a horseman, Rudy is renowned for not only his riding talents but for . . ." She didn't click to the page but skipped to the next headline: "A Clinic with Rudy Bridges, Equestrian Instructor." The article began, "Rudy is an approved instructor for the National Trainer Certification Program . . ." She skipped to the next headline: "At Home with Rudy Bridges." It began, "From what was once a simple ranch, Equestrian Pages now brings a host of world-class trainers and competitors right to your home . . ." The next: "Rudy Bridges, the Heart of a Horseman." The next: "Perfect the Automatic Release with Rudy Bridges." And on and on.

She looked over the images: Rudy laughing, what had to be his résumé shot, a portrait that looked like it was from the 1990s, Rudy as a clown . . .

She inhaled sharply. She peered closer. Yes, there he was as a rodeo clown, complete with a ridiculous patchwork outfit, a scarecrowlike straw hat, bright-red suspenders, the whole bit. "Interesting," she murmured.

She closed her laptop, gathered her books, and hurried out, smirking.

As Elaine left the student lounge, Anya entered and went straight to Josh. "I think I have a problem," she moaned at him.

Josh looked up from his laptop, automatically going into Tease Mode. "Freaking out about the competish?"

Anya's expression of dismay turned to one of confusion. "Competish . . . sh . . . shion? Competition! Oh, I'll worry about that later. Right now, I don't have a dress for the gala!"

Josh leaned back in his chair, clueless as to why Anya would be coming to him but rather delighted that she had. He liked her. She had such a strange sense of humor. "Is this one of those girl things where *I don't have a dress* means *I have, like, six hundred in my closet, but I just want to go shopping?*" When Anya shot him an odd look, he explained, "I have sisters."

Poor Anya was totally lost. "I don't have sisters. Or six hundred dresses. Is that what you're asking? I'm not quite sure what you're asking."

Josh laughed. "You're funny. Not funny ha-ha, but there's something different about you."

Anya gulped. "I was homeschooled!"

"Ohhh. That *so* makes sense." He winked at her knowingly.

Anya sat down and, without realizing it, gave him big puppy eyes. "Oh, please help."

The effect on Josh was instantaneous. Tease Mode switched to Serious Guy Helping Pretty Girl Mode as he brought up his search engine, typed in "party dresses," and hit the Search button. He swiveled the laptop around so that Anya could see the screen. It displayed picture after picture of cute dresses and where to get them. "The beauty of online shopping," he said. "Pick a dress, choose overnight shipping, and boom, you're done."

It was as if Anya had never before seen such a thing. She took in all the dress choices and cried, "Thank you!" Then, to his total surprise (and Josh didn't surprise easily), she threw her arms around him and hugged him tight. "Thankyouthankyouthankyou! This changes everything!"

It certainly did for Josh. He had just rescued a damsel in distress, and she'd given him a very nice hug. Very nice indeed. He could get used to this. . . .

Chapter 10

PLAYING GAMES

E laine, fully dressed for riding, led her chestnut gelding, Thunder, who was fully tacked up, out of the stable and toward the practice ring. It was time for her to take matters into her own hands. She wasn't going to lose to Beatrice Bates because of some rodeo clown.

Unfortunately, the rodeo clown was standing in the stable courtyard watching her. "You taking that saddle for a walk?" Rudy asked. "Because I thought my instructions were pretty clear. No riding today."

Elaine mentally prepared for an argument. Disagreeing with Rudy didn't bother her in the least, but disagreeing with a teacher did. Her record at Covington was spotless. She was a model student.

She did not cause trouble. But this was one issue that she couldn't ignore any longer. "Look," she said, trying to maintain a respectful attitude, "I don't like breaking the rules. But in order to win, we have to train properly."

Rudy tipped his Stetson farther back on his forehead. "My training is proper. Just different proper."

"With all due respect, sir, I'm simply not prepared to have that judged by a rodeo clown."

Instead of seeming insulted, as Elaine had expected, Rudy gave a small nod, his expression thoughtful. "Well, yeah, it's true. On my way up, I've taken just about every job that involves horses. That's how you meet the best horse people. And you get to watch them make mistakes." He let that sink in. "Now you, for example, can't execute a balanced figure eight. Couldn't do it if there was a gold medal in it for you."

Elaine felt the hairs on the back of her neck rise. "That is simply not true."

"Yeah. It is. And this *clown* can help you fix it."

Elaine bit her lip and thought of Beatrice Bates. Maybe Rudy wasn't challenging her, putting her down, or insulting her. Could it be that he genuinely wanted to help?

This rodeo clown might have something worth-while to teach her after all.

Out in the arena, Kit worked with TK, who had finally calmed down and accepted that the bridle was on to stay. It was a good start. A teeny-weeny one, but a good one.

"And now," she said, putting as much enthusiasm as she could into her voice, "we walk in a circle for no particular reason!" She started in a circle backward, hands beckoning to TK. "Come on, boy! It's super fun—I promise!"

TK apparently thought circles were dull. He refused to follow or even acknowledge Kit's voice. Kit returned to him and scratched his forehead. "We have to pass tests," she told him sternly. "This is totally serious, so let me help you. Okay?"

TK grunted.

"We're going to play a little game. It's easy. It's called Simon Says." She called back to Will and Nav, who were leaning against the rails "helping" her. "Hey, turn on the music! It'll help him relax!"

Like lightning, both boys grabbed for Kit's phone, which was on the top rail. Nav got it first. Will didn't exactly frown, but his jaw tightened visibly as Nav turned the device on.

Kit stared deep into TK's big brown eyes. "Simon says go right!" she said, again putting as much enthusiasm and cheer into her voice as she could muster. While dance music played from her phone, she did a happy little dance step to the right.

TK followed at a walk.

Encouraged, Kit said, "Simon says go left!" and she danced to the left, throwing her whole body into it.

TK began to catch her energy. He gave a little hop and followed her left, his tail swishing.

"Simon says go right again!" Kit laughed, dancing to the right.

TK followed, not quite dancing, but his steps were more energetic. He grunted and neighed, tossing his head to the music.

Nav smiled, charmed by Kit's antics. Will raised an eyebrow. That eyebrow spoke volumes to Nav. "I thought you were off girls," he commented drily. Will just glanced at him, then turned back to the spectacle of the girl and the dancing horse.

After he had successfully danced right and left several times, Kit scratched TK's forehead. "Good boy!" she praised him. "Now Simon says jump. It's easy. Don't worry. I'll show you how." Thudding across the damp grass in her big Wellington boots, she ran at one of the low jumps in the arena and leaped over it. She spun around to watch TK follow her.

He wasn't following. In fact, he was doing a very good impression of a statue.

"Come on, TK! Come on, you can do it!"

In a burst of motion, TK cleared the jump and didn't stop until he was at Kit's side. She laughed in delight, while Nav and Will applauded.

None of them were aware that Lady Covington was watching from her office window.

Elaine wanted to scream.

While Rudy pretended to be busy doing something nearby, she attempted to bond with Thunder. "Hey, Thunder, how's your day going? Is your feed good? Mmm, delicious alfalfa!"

Thunder didn't even do her the favor of looking at her. He gazed over her head at nothing. He didn't even stop chewing.

She slumped.

"Walk the course with him," Rudy suggested. "A simple figure eight. Let him follow."

Elaine put her hands on her hips. "That's something four-year-olds do with ponies. I'm his *rider*."

"If my way fails, I'll resign," Rudy offered.

Elaine brightened. "Really?"

"Ah, no."

Elaine scowled.

"But just try it. And close your eyes. Close them," Rudy repeated when she shook her head no. "Now. Tight together."

"What is this supposed to accomplish?" Elaine grumbled, but she closed her eyes and began the figure eight with Thunder at her side. "This is ridiculous. I feel ridiculous!"

"Just think about the pattern," Rudy said, almost hypnotically. "The figure eight."

Elaine gritted her teeth. "I've known what a figure eight looks like since nursery," she huffed as she came around the second loop of the eight. "I need to *ride*!" She stumbled a little and opened her eyes.

"That!" Rudy cried, pointing at her. "What's that? Why did you stop? Every time you come around that turn, you hesitate. Why?"

"I don't." Elaine stood still. She pursed her lips.

"Look," said Rudy, "everything you feel, you transfer to your horse. Frustration, love, anger, embarrassment, all of it. Thunder feels that, too. What happened?"

"It's nothing."

"Okay. Good luck against Bates. I'll be on a plane back west."

Reluctantly, Elaine confessed, "I dropped a stirrup. Last year. My foot slipped out, I don't know why, and then I lost my balance and fell in the dirt." She wanted to look anywhere but at her teacher. "It was awful. . . ."

"Why?"

Shrugging helplessly, she insisted, "It just happened!"

"No, no, why did you slip? The wrong boots, bad breakfast . . . a boy?" Elaine's expression turned to stone. "Look, let all that embarrassment go, all right? It's just dust. All you need to do is think about the perfect eight and Thunder." He smiled at her.

Elaine didn't quite smile back, but the corners of her lips lifted a tiny bit. She rubbed Thunder's neck affectionately. Rodeo clown, indeed!

An hour later, Kit was in Rudy's office when Lady Covington walked in. Kit had never seen the head-mistress in the stables before, but of course, it was silly to think she never went there. Kit was not happy to see her. Visits from Lady Covington rarely meant good news.

"Groundwork has never been a part of any dressage competition that I have ever seen," the head-mistress told her. Her meaning was clear enough: groundwork was not a part of dressage, period.

"But did you see TK walk after me?" Kit asked. "That has to be a victory, right? He just does things a little differently."

Lady Covington did not agree. "Clearly you need time to learn even the basics. Based on that obvious fact, I've come up with a contract."

Kit's heart leaped. "Does that mean he stays?"

"You will have to prove that both you and TK are worthy of our riding program. I expect you to be riding by the end of the month, and by the midterm event, I expect you to be out on the field competing with the rest of your classmates. Or we can go back to the original plan. I'm sure that TK will fetch a very good price at auction."

"No!" Kit cried. "I—I'll sign."

Lady Covington opened one of the file folders in her arms and flipped several papers over until she came to the page she wanted. "Right here." She held out a pen.

"Oh." Kit gulped. "You weren't joking?"

"Joking is for the lazy and the light-minded. Sign there, please."

Kit took the pen and scratched her name quickly on the document. She figured she should have read it first, but her father was watching, and Lady Covington was putting pressure on her just by existing. Nothing else mattered but that she get her name on that contract so TK wouldn't disappear overnight.

She handed the pen back, and Lady Covington closed her file folder with a satisfied nod. "Carry on," she said, and left.

Kit slowly turned around to face her dad sitting behind his desk. "I can't believe I just signed my name to that thing," she said, plopping down into a chair. "And now I'm going to have to *do* that thing."

"And you will," said Rudy. "You're Kit Bridges. I've never known anyone as determined as you." He started to laugh, but a shadow darkened his features. "Except . . ."

"Mom?"

Rudy's smile returned. "Speaking of which . . ." He got up and tossed his coat aside. Under it was a large box, which he placed on his desk. "I thought you might need a little something for the gala."

Kit opened the box and gasped, recognizing the pattern on the neat bundle of material inside. Reverently she picked it up. "This was her dress." She held it up against herself in wonder. The dress was a vintage mini from the 1980s, totally boho chic, Kit's signature style. Of course, she'd adopted the style from her mother in the first place. "I've been so busy with TK, I didn't even think about what I was going to wear." Kit raced around the desk and gave her father a hug. "Thanks for the save, Dad!"

Chapter 11

THE GALA

The van from Bingham Academy arrived, turned a wide circle in the gravel driveway, and came to a halt before the main doors.

When Beatrice Bates stepped out, Elaine and her posse were there to greet her. "Bates," she said in a flat tone.

Bates was slightly taller than Elaine and dressed in Bingham's red-and-blue uniform. Other than the different school colors, though, the two girls could have been sisters. Both had trim athletic bodies, they stood straight and proud, their hair was light, their skin clear, and their attitudes snarky. As her own squad exited the van and took up positions that exactly mirrored the positions of Elaine's friends, Bates greeted her nemesis in an equally flat tone: "Whiltshire."

So began the Whiltshire-Bates War. It wasn't on the official list of weekend events, but it was an event nonetheless. A very serious one.

Elaine began the verbal duel portion of the war with a lunge: "Nice try," she told Bates, "but photos aren't going to psych me out. Next time, try harder."

Bates's riposte was to sneer and say, "Oh, I'm just getting started."

"'The mind is everything. What you think, you become.'"

"'Success is ten percent inspiration and ninety percent perspiration.'"

"That explains the smell."

Bates's lips quivered. She had nothing.

Score! Elaine turned her back on her nemesis and walked away.

That evening as Josh ambled innocently along the corridor of the main building, he was nearly bowled over by a frantic Anya. "Josh!" she cried. "Josh! Josh!"

"Whoa!" he said, steadying her as she stumbled to a halt. "Slow your roll there!"

"The dresses," Anya panted. "They just arrived!" She held them up. "I can't tell what's suitable, and I can't find Kit, so—help!"

Now Josh understood. "Is this why you weren't in the stables today?"

"I'm so stressed! I put the wrong address on the package, and then I had to go into the village to pick it up, and then I missed the shuttle bus back!" She shoved the dresses at him for inspection. "What do you think?"

He looked from one dress to the other. Both were red, but the one on the right . . . "Dude," he said, "is that for you or Lady C?"

Insulted, Anya grumbled, "It looked different on the thumbnail."

He just shook his head. "Next."

Anya held the other dress out. It was simple, unadorned, but well tailored. It would surely look great on her. "Oh, yeah," said Josh. "Totally nailed it."

"Are you one hundred percent sure?"

"Is this a test?"

"Kind of. For me, anyway."

"Then you totally passed."

Anya gave a happy squeal, and Josh grinned. The gala was going to start in a couple of hours. He was looking forward to seeing Anya in that dress.

Kit took her time getting ready for the gala, trying on various bracelets and necklaces and messing with her hair. In the end, she decided to let her mother's dress do all the talking and settled for a simple metallic beaded necklace and her usual hairstyle. Shoes were another matter. Those had to make a statement, and the statement was "Cowgirl!" Her bright red Corral boots did the trick.

In a fit of fatherly adorableness, Rudy had asked if he could escort her from Rose Cottage to the main building, where the gala was taking place. So once she was ready, Kit met him outside the cottage, and they ambled their way arm in arm to the door of the dining hall, where they paused to survey the scene.

The dining hall had been transformed into a wonderland of glittering lights and decorations. Dance music thumped so loudly that the chandeliers in the hallway vibrated with each beat. Students from Covington and Bingham were happily chatting and munching nibbles. A few couples were already out on the dance floor. The only thing that looked odd to Kit was the fact that all the guys were wearing James

Bond tuxedos with bow ties. She was used to school dances with the boys in denim and cowboy boots.

Before stepping into the room, Rudy said to her, "The dress suits you."

"Thanks," Kit said. She knew he'd been dying to say that since they'd left Rose Cottage, but her dad always got shy when it came to giving compliments. Kit also knew that seeing the dress had to be hard for him. She couldn't express how much she loved him for not only keeping it but for giving it to her for the gala. She was tempted to hug him, but hugging your own dad just wasn't something you did at a dance, so she opted for saying, "You look good, too."

He did exactly what she expected: he gazed down at himself and muttered, "I'm counting the seconds till I can get out of this rig." He tugged at his teacher's tie, which he was required to wear, for the umpteenth time. Kit held back a giggle.

Nav appeared before them, smiling his ever-suave smile. "Mr. Bridges," he formally greeted Rudy. "It is my honor to take care of your daughter this evening."

"What . . . are you talking about?" Rudy asked him cautiously while Kit thought, *Take care of? Take care of?*

Nav had no time to explain himself as Elaine, looking cute in a sleek green dress, stepped up to Rudy and held up her mobile. The screen showed a close-up photo of her somehow taken while she'd been walking Thunder in the figure eight with her eyes closed. It wasn't as bad as the gap-toothed childhood photo, but she obviously considered it to be yet another embarrassing insult. "She sent it to everyone!" she complained.

Rudy was clueless. "Who?"

"Bates! That smug blond troll needs to lose! That is why you are going to talk me through my strategy again. We compete in the morning!" She led Rudy away.

He seemed to go willingly enough, probably knowing he'd get no peace until he could calm her down, but Kit knew he wasn't happy about it. The Whiltshire-Bates War was getting on everyone's nerves.

Nav took this opportunity to move closer to Kit. "Would you like some punch, Katherine?" he asked her as if fetching punch was the most fantastic thing he could ever do.

"Uh, *Kit's* fine," she replied. "And no, I'm okay. Oh, look, there's Will. Hey, Will!" She waved at him, hoping he would join them, but Will took one look at Nav, gave Kit a small smile, and moved quickly—in the other direction. Confused, Kit was about to call him again when Anya arrived.

Kit took in the simple yet elegant red dress on her roomie while Anya gawked at Kit's outfit. "You look amazing!" they both squealed at each other.

"Thanks. It was my mom's," Kit said.

"It's lovely." Gesturing to her own dress, Anya declared with pride, "I ordered this online because that's a thing that I can do."

"Yup!" Josh slid over and draped his arm across Anya's shoulders. "All by herself. Zero drama." He and Anya exchanged a high five.

With a sudden "Shall we?" Nav whisked Kit off to the dance floor. They danced for a while with Josh and Anya then split into groups. Kit looked around for Will again and spotted him coming back in from the hallway. She started to say hello, but he just swept on by, acknowledging her with a noncommittal nod.

Kit turned helplessly to Anya. "Will is completely not speaking to me."

"I noticed that," Anya said. "I don't understand it. And Nav—"

"Nav just keeps bringing me punch. I've told him I'm not thirsty, like, a billion times."

As if on cue, Nav danced his way across the floor to Kit with yet another cup of punch, which he handed to her with a beaming smile. Seeing that she and Anya were deep in discussion, he danced away again.

The two girls watched in complete confusion. "Wait," Anya said. "Nav didn't ask to escort you here tonight, did he?"

"No," Kit answered. "I mean, I don't think so. I mean, half the time I don't understand a word any of you are saying!" She paused. "He said something like the gala is fun, and he wondered if I would consider—"

Anya's jaw dropped. "That's very clearly an invitation. You're very clearly his date!"

Kit was so shocked by this that when Lady Covington entered the dining hall and happened to lock eyes with her for a split second, Kit waved a little too cheerily. The headmistress continued on her way while Kit quietly freaked. "I just waved at Lady C!"

"I saw," said Anya. "Why would you do that?"

"I don't know. I panicked!"

"Well, you have to go talk to her now. Otherwise, it's unforgivably rude."

Great. Either Kit cozied up to Lady Covington at a school dance, of all places, or she would add Unforgivable Rudeness to her list of faults in the headmistress's eyes. It wasn't that she disliked the woman, but what could they possibly talk about?

She found the headmistress standing by the drinks table. "Lady Covington," Kit said nervously. "Gotta say, you're looking wickedly stylin' this evening."

Lady Covington donned a gracious smile. "Whatever language you're speaking, I don't understand you."

"There's a lot of that going around. So, uh, nice night. Nice party. I—I am so nervous. . . ." She gulped down some punch, and when she still couldn't think of anything to say, she drank some more. When her glass ran dry, she blurted out, "And thirsty! I get nervous when I'm thirsty." No, that wasn't right. *Thirsty when I'm nervous . . .*"

"Where did you get your dress?"

Kit froze. Was the headmistress helping her out here, or was she actually interested? Or was this just one of those general questions English adults asked teenagers at parties? *I'll never get the hang of this country!* she thought. Then again, did it matter? She should accept any help she could get at the moment. "Oh, do you like it?" she asked, trying not to sound like her fist was about to crush her empty punch glass. "It was my mom's."

Apparently intrigued by this answer, Lady Covington looked Kit up and down to take in the dress's details more carefully. But she made no further comment.

"Look, I just want to say thank you." That was surprising. Kit had no such desire. But once she said it, she realized it was true. "Not everyone would give me this chance with TK, and you did. And that's really cool." She tried to look grateful.

Either Lady Covington was amused by Kit's awkwardness or she was genuinely touched by the declaration of thanks. It was hard to tell, but at least the headmistress's smile warmed up a little. "Well, I'm glad that you find it *cool.* Enjoy your evening."

Kit didn't understand the dismissal until Nav spoke from right behind her. "Shall we dance?"

It was the punch thing all over again—he kept asking her to dance! This time, though, Kit actually wanted to. Something in her heart brightened, and it felt good. It felt really good. "Let's all dance!" she cried, and happily lost herself in the music.

Later that night, when the dance was over and everyone had gone to bed, Kit tiptoed into the stables to see a special someone.

"Hi, boy," she greeted TK, entering his stall. "I stole you some snacks from the buffet." She opened her purse, pulled out several baby carrots, and held them out.

She giggled as her sensitive palm first registered TK's hot puffs of breath and the tickle of his chin whiskers. Since his eyes were so far up on his face, he couldn't actually see the carrots. He had to smell them first and locate them with his whiskers. Then his soft, rubbery lips brushed against her skin as they picked the carrots up and drew them into his mouth. The most wonderful sound followed, the *crunch-crunch* of big horse teeth munching. It was so loud, it sounded like a recording of a human chewing with a microphone pressed against their neck.

TK nuzzled her as he chewed. "How was my night?" Kit pretended to hear. "It was great, thank you for asking. How about the dress? Do you like it? It was my mom's."

TK, still chewing, gave a little snort.

Kit took it as approval. "I really wish she could have been here tonight," she went on, thinking that if she had been able to talk to her mom, she might not have made such a fool of herself with Nav and all that punch. "A guy asked me out on a date, and I didn't even know it! How does a girl end up on a date that she doesn't even know she's on?"

TK's whinny seemed to say, "It turned out well, though, didn't it?"

"Yeah," Kit admitted, "but here's the thing . . . I think I like someone else. And you"—she patted the gelding's neck—"haven't been making his life any easier lately. So promise you'll behave yourself tomorrow."

TK's only response was to nudge her purse, looking for more carrots.

There was another response, however, one that Kit did not see. Will had wandered into the barn in time to overhear her confession to TK, and he couldn't help but hope that her "someone else" was him. It sure sounded like it.

He smiled.

Chapter 12

DRESSAGE DISASTER

W elcome to the annual Covington versus Bingham event," said the announcer over the loudspeaker.

Covington's courtyard was full of proud parents, eager contestants, perfectly groomed and tacked horses, and a maze of trucks and horse trailers. To everyone's delight, the sun shone bright in a clear blue sky, a rare state of weather in England, and it put everyone in high spirits.

The event itself was taking place in the school's indoor arena, where the audience bleachers had been divided into two groups: the Covington side in blue and the Bingham side in red. Kit had learned that the day's three contests were a kind of equestrian triathlon known as eventing. Dressage had taken place that morning. It was a test of precision riding designed to demonstrate the obedience of a horse and the control of its rider. Cross-country, which would take place last, was a test of a horse's speed, endurance, and jumping abilities outdoors. Show jumping, which was taking place now, was an arena event requiring horse and rider to complete a specific jump course with as few mistakes as possible. These tests didn't sound particularly difficult, but Kit knew they took a lot of training and practice.

For the show jumping phase, jumps of various sizes and heights had been arranged around the arena floor. Sitting next to Rudy on the Covington side, Kit watched in suspense as Elaine navigated the course astride Thunder. As much as Kit often disagreed with the blond perfectionist, she couldn't complain about Elaine's riding skills. The girl rode exquisitely, now guiding Thunder up and over the last jump with full control, perfect style, and no mishaps. She walked him out of the ring amid applause, pausing by the stands to wait for the announcement of her score.

"Good clean ride," Rudy said to her. "Tight corners."

Elaine beamed. "Thanks, Coach. You know, you're not a bad teacher, for a rodeo clown."

Kit couldn't believe what she was hearing. *She just called my dad a clown! In public!* Well, it had been true for a time, but still.

Rudy only laughed.

Over on the Bingham side, Beatrice Bates stood up to address her nemesis. "It'll be tough to beat my score."

Elaine raised her chin. "Not that tough." With a glance at Rudy, she added, "Thunder and I had a conversation first. We talked about our mutual goals."

Now Rudy looked downright proud. "Atta girl," he praised her, making Elaine actually blush.

"Elaine Whiltshire, The Covington Academy," came the announcer's voice over the loudspeaker. "Clear round. That puts her in first."

A roar rose from the Covington audience. A few reluctant claps came from the Bingham side. Beatrice Bates folded her arms across her chest as if to hold in her disappointment. "My school's still leading."

"Perhaps," said Elaine. "But Anya Patel's up next. Prepare to lose."

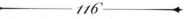

"Anya Patel," the announcer said. "Calling Anya Patel to the ring."

Everyone turned to watch Anya come riding into the arena on Just Ducky, her beautiful chestnut gelding.

But no Anya appeared.

Seconds passed, and still no Anya.

Kit leaped to her feet and raced into the tack room, where she found her roommate completely unready for her turn in the ring. She didn't even have her competition uniform on yet. Just Ducky's tack lay scattered on a table and the floor, and Anya was in a complete panic.

"You're supposed to be out there!" Kit cried.

"All my shirts were dirty, and then I couldn't find my formal breeches, and then I forgot my bridle wasn't ready and—"

"Why didn't you do this before?"

Anya's hands flapped wildly. "I don't know! There was the whole business with the gala dress and, and usually—" Her voice rose to a high-pitched wail as she finished. "Well, usually I get some help!"

"Anya Patel," the announcer called again. "Final call for Anya Patel."

Out in the audience, Lady Covington turned to Rudy. "Where is she?"

Rudy had no answer.

"Last call for Anya Patel. Begin immediately or be disqualified."

Anya's distress was wound as tight as it could go. At the word *disqualified* she simply froze, hands in mid-flap. Then all her energy drained away, and with an anguished groan, she completely deflated. It was too late. It was over.

She was disqualified.

After all three eventing phases were over, Anya found herself alone in the tack room with Lady Covington. Both stared at the results displayed on the computer.

Elaine, of course, had claimed first place, with Beatrice Bates in a close second. Nav came in third, and Kiki Welch, from Bingham, scored fourth. Jilly Jones, also from Bingham, had taken fifth place. Covington had lost the event overall.

Anya's name did appear on the board. In red. With no points at all.

"And that concludes today's competition," the announcer was saying on the computer. "Jilly Jones is in fifth place, and Anya Patel of Covington has been disqualified."

Lady Covington rounded on Anya. "Disqualified!" she said with disdain. "How do you simply miss your stadium round?"

Anya flinched. "I'm sorry, Lady Covington."

"Is Covington proving to be too much for you?"

"No, Lady Covington!" Anya tried not to look desperate. "It won't happen again!"

"No," Lady Covington declared hotly. "It won't."

Anya stood shaking in shame as Lady Covington stalked away. Then she hurried out where she had tied Just Ducky up and led him into the stables. She may have missed the competition, but she had gotten herself together enough to ride the course afterward.

Kit was waiting for her near Just Ducky's stall. "You crushed that jump course," she said, trying to make Anya feel better. "You were awesome! That should make you feel better, right?"

Anya silently tied Just Ducky outside the stall door and began to remove his tack.

Kit refused to give up. "Like, how big a deal is it that you were disqualified from the competition?"

"It's huge," Anya said in a small voice. "I'm humiliated."

"But still, you really did rock those jumps. You should change Just Ducky's name. Call him Jet. Or Soar! Or . . . what do they call those horses that have wings?"

"Imaginary?" Will offered, appearing with a bale of hay.

"Pegasus!" Kit suddenly remembered. "That's what you two looked like! Serious altitude. I'm surprised you don't have seagulls in your teeth." She gave Will a meaningful glare.

He got the message. "Uh, good job, Anya," he said, setting the hay down.

Anya lost it. *"It doesn't matter!"* she shouted.

Kit jumped in surprise. Will automatically put his hand on Just Ducky's flank, since Anya's outburst startled him. He soothed the horse while Anya continued to vent. "I got disqualified! I let the team down! I let my family down! I let my horse down!"

Anya's uncharacteristic outburst only made Kit more determined to make her feel better. She manipulated Just Ducky's big lips to make it look like he was talking. "'I think you're the greatest! And you smell yummy!'"

It just made Anya bury her face in her hands. "Can we *please* stop pretending it's okay?"

Kit admitted defeat and backed away.

"Do you want me to take him for a cooldown?" Will asked Anya. He took her horse's lead.

She was near tears. "Yes. Please. That." She fled the stables.

An hour after breakfast the next morning, the students were instructed via intercom to return to the dining hall. Kit filed in with the rest of her peers, knowing that some kind of unpleasant dressing-down was coming. The teachers were already somberly seated on the raised dais. Lady Covington stood at a central podium. The breakfast tables had been replaced with rows of chairs, so Kit chose one and sat. Josh settled down next to her. They exchanged nervous glances as Lady Covington began to speak.

"The problem is not that we lost to Bingham Academy this weekend," the headmistress intoned with unconcealed annoyance. "An honest loss is something to be celebrated. It's something that we can all learn from. However, this was less a loss than it was a *humiliation*. Do any of you remember whose name is on the school gate? The crest? The riding uniform? *My* name. Covington. And Covington has been humiliated. As you all wear this name, you should all feel humiliated, too — with a few notable exceptions." She zeroed in on Elaine. "Miss Whiltshire, congratulations on your first place. Well done."

Elaine dared a smile.

"Mr. Andrada."

Nav sucked in a nervous breath.

"I enjoyed your jump round immensely, as did the judges, apparently. Good show."

He relaxed again, tried to smile, but couldn't quite make it.

"Many of you need to recommit to your training. Strive for excellence . . ."

As Lady Covington continued to speak, Josh leaned over to Kit and whispered, "Where's Anya?"

"I don't know," Kit whispered back. "I didn't see her at all this morning."

"Miss Bridges!"

Kit jumped in her seat.

"You are not exempt from listening to me despite the fact that you failed to ride. You ought to be working even harder than the others, given that rather embarrassing fact."

Kit knew that anything less than a polite answer would spell disaster, so she said, "Absolutely. I will." And nothing else.

That seemed to please the headmistress, who concluded her speech with, "In short, I expect the rest of the year to be, quite simply, *better*. Dismissed."

Everyone quietly, almost fearfully, filed out of the dining hall. Kit followed them until she heard Lady Covington say, "Mr. Bridges? Please meet me in my office as soon as possible."

"Right away, Lady Covington," Rudy replied, casting a pained glance at Kit. She returned a sympathetic *ouch* face.

When the room was almost clear, Lady Covington's manner relaxed. Heaving a long-suffering sigh, she said to Sally, "I fear that I am bound to spend most of the rest of my life managing the Bridges." Her tone suggested that she was making a small joke, but under the circumstances, Sally knew better than to laugh.

It was too early for class, so Kit returned to her dorm room. "Anya?"

The room was empty.

Or was it? Earlier that morning while she had been getting dressed, Kit had thought that Anya's bed was empty. But these dorm beds were super-fluffy. A person as petite as Anya could hide under there, unnoticed, couldn't they?

She yanked the covers back. There lay Anya. Her hands flew up to cover her face.

"Have you been in there all morning?" Kit asked her. "The whole time I was getting ready?"

"I'm actually not here," Anya mumbled.

"Huh. Weird." Kit perched on the edge of the bed. "Not sure who I'm going to share this delicious pastry thingamajiggy with, then."

That got Anya's attention. She peeked through her fingers at the delicate sweet roll sitting on Kit's napkin. Several telltale dark blotches revealed what it was. "They had *pain au chocolat* at breakfast?"

"Yup," Kit said. "Apparently *pan oh chocolate* is available only to those who actually make it to the Assembly of Doom. And in about two seconds, I'm going to devour this. One . . . two . . ."

Anya bolted upright and grabbed the pastry.

Kit wanted to laugh—Anya picking at the pastry looked so much like a hungry squirrel nibbling nuts. But she was on a mission to make her roomie feel better, not worse. "Now, if I can get you to leave this room, we might be able to find some delicious milk shakes!"

Mouth full, Anya shook her head no.

"Some cute new boots?"

Headshake no.

"Some cute new boys?"

Anya's words came out almost in a whisper. "I can never show my face in the ring again. Or in school. I've never done anything quite so awful before."

Kit shrugged. "You messed up. So? It happens."

"I wasn't prepared for my dressage test," Anya lamented. "I didn't have any of my clothes ready or my tack or my mind! None of it! It was horrible. . . ."

Kit had a sudden inspiration. "My friend Charlie and I used to play this game called Best/Worst. It would always make us feel better because it was highly unlikely that either scenario would come true. So—what is the worst thing that happens if you leave this room?"

"Nothing, because I'm never leaving it." With that, Anya and her *pain au chocolat* disappeared under the covers again.

Kit pulled the duvet back down. "What is the *best* thing that happens if you leave this room?"

Anya popped back upright and said glumly, "Spaceships touch down and wipe out everyone's memories so that I can start all over again."

"Great! Maybe the aliens can sweep up Lady C while they're here." Kit's attempt at humor almost won a smile, but not quite. "Come on," Kit urged, getting up and bringing Anya's riding uniform to her. "I bet Ducky would love to go for a run."

Ride

KIT MEETS COVINGTON

Will, Nav, Rudy, Kit, Anya, Josh, and Elaine

TK welcomes Kit to Covington.

Kit and TK

The Covington Academy for the Equestrian Arts

Nav and Josh make a plan.

Elaine takes first place.

Josh rides Whistler.

Kit and Rudy meet Lady C.

Kit

Elaine

Will

Nav

Josh

Anya

Elaine shows Kit what's wrong.

Kit and Rudy cheer the Covington team.

"Okay," agreed Anya. She pushed her uniform back at Kit. "So *you* take him."

Oh, dear. This was not the direction Kit wanted the conversation to go. "I—I can't," she said.

"You have to get on a horse, or you'll lose TK." Anya paused. "Best/Worst."

It was only fair for Kit to give an answer. "Best," she said, creating the image in her mind, "I hop on TK, and we clear all of the jumps like superstars on the first try. With my hands up in the air like this." And she threw both arms up in the air like she was riding a roller coaster.

Anya actually smiled. "Worst?"

Kit didn't have to create an image for that. It had been haunting her since coming to Covington. "My fear overpowers all of my other senses, and I pass out in the dirt. Face-first. And the video goes viral." She frowned at the mental image, but Anya's cute giggle broke through. Kit took advantage of it and pushed the riding uniform back at her. "Come on, get dressed."

The suggestion just made Anya bow her head. "I'm taking a sickie," she announced, and flopped back on her pillows, pulling the duvet over her head.

She became nothing more than a suspicious lump in the bed again.

Kit let it go. Anya just needed time, right?

Right?

Chapter 13

GRACE KELLY AND MRS. WHISKERS

Nav was trying to study—he really was. He sat comfortably cross-legged on his bed, textbook and notebook open on his lap, pen in hand, his mind clear of distractions—

No, that wasn't true. About every three minutes, his roommate (Will, of all people) tossed a wadded piece of paper at the trash can. Sometimes it went in. Sometimes it didn't. Either way, the noise of Will crunching each sheet of paper into a wad followed by the sound of said wad hitting the trash can (either on its way in or bouncing its way out) disrupted Nav's train of thought. How could one possibly improve one's intellectual abilities in such a hectic environment?

It wasn't bad enough that Will was, by any standards known on Earth, untidy. It was the fact that he didn't stop at untidy. He dived all the way into filthy and continued right up to the burning edges of toxic waste dump. While Nav's side of the room was spotless—bed tidily made, clothing neatly put away, floor clear, furniture surfaces not only clutter free but dusted and polished—Will's side of the room displayed all the charm of a bar brawl—clothes strewn everywhere, dresser and table overflowing with piled-up junk, bed unmade, posters half hanging off the walls. And to top it off, Will lay in his unmade bed fully dressed and listening to loud music on headphones while reading some magazine or other and eating crisps. A bag of crisps! In bed! Getting greasy crumbs all over his sheets and pillows! And he *didn't care*!

It was enough to give Nav nightmares.

When yet another piece of paper got wadded up and thrown, Nav listened for the results. He didn't hear the sound of paper-in-can but of paper-on-floor. "You missed," he stated. He enjoyed stating the obvious. It annoyed Will to no end.

"I'll get it later," Will said grumpily.

"If you're going to act like a pig, William, you will soon become one."

"Did you know that pigs are very smart?" Will shot back. "Anyway, I know exactly where everything is." He gestured at his mountains of clutter. "It's my system."

Nav had had enough. "Either you pick it up, or you get better aim."

Will adjusted his headphones. "Oh, sorry, can't hear you. Guitar solo." And just to annoy Nav even more, he began to hum, very badly, along with the tune.

Okay, two could play this game. Nav ripped out a page of his notebook, crunched it up, and tossed it. Perfect shot right into the trash can! "That's how it's done," he said with a superior smile, adding, "*Andrada* style."

He should have known better. Before Nav could even think about resuming his studies, Will crunched up another page and scored. "That's not so hard."

Nav tried again and missed. "Two out of three?" he suggested.

Will gestured for him to go ahead.

Nav tossed and scored.

Will wadded up a paper, tossed, and missed. "Three out of five?"

Nav knew to quit while he was ahead. "No, thank you. I've got some tack to clean."

"You serious?" Will leaned back. "I got all mine cleaned after the event yesterday."

That sounded like a challenge to Nav. "Are you saying that you're faster than me?"

"Hear what you want to hear," Will replied. "*Andrada* style."

Oh, yes, that was a challenge. "Let the games begin!" Nav said, and he hustled out the door without looking back. He didn't have to. He knew that Will would follow. This wasn't the first time this had happened, after all.

Kit was sharing some quality time with TK. She had just given him a thorough grooming in his stall and was now putting the equipment back into her grooming box.

"It's so different here," she chatted, placing several different currycombs into the box along with a soft face brush and hoof-pick. "I keep having major misunderstandings. So I've started a list." She pulled TK's tail brush out of her back pocket and dropped it in the box. "*It's in the boot* means something's in the trunk of a car, not in my footwear." She flapped a couple of rags clean and dropped those into the box along with a sponge. "A *fizzy drink* is soda pop, so I can stop giving Will weird looks when he offers me one."

She checked around the stall and located the pulling comb, a tool used to thin a horse's mane so that it lay down more smoothly and was easier to braid for shows. She hadn't yet ridden TK in a show, but since that was the plan, she figured she should use one on him. TK nickered as she placed the pulling comb into the box. She pretended that he'd asked her a question, to which she replied, "There wasn't even anybody in class to laugh with me about it. Anya is *still* in bed." She picked up the grooming box and placed it outside the stall so that she'd remember to take it back to the tack room.

Her dad approached with a wheelbarrow full of hay. "Hey, kiddo," he greeted her. "What are you up to?"

Kit instantly recognized his tone. He was trying to sound casual, but underneath that light greeting was a question she didn't want to hear and *especially* didn't want to answer. So she said flippantly, "Oh, just teaching TK to throw down like Jay Z."

"Really."

"Well, I figure if I can get him spitting mad rhymes, Lady C will have to let me keep him."

Rudy was in no mood for jokes. "If you want to keep him, you're going to have to ride him. Otherwise he'll be gone so fast it'll make your head spin. Lady C's not in the mood to compromise."

So much for avoiding the topic. "You don't have to be so blunt."

"Push yourself a little. You need to get on that horse *yesterday*."

Over in the tack room, Nav and Will were in a race to finish cleaning their saddles. They'd reached the polishing stage, standing side by side, each of their saddles on a sturdy wooden saddle rack while they madly rubbed with polishing rags. They tried to ignore that they could hear Kit and Rudy talking.

"My knees get wobbly," they heard Kit say, "and my stomach starts to flop around like I'm on the world's nastiest roller coaster."

"It feels bigger than it is," came Rudy's fatherly voice as the boys continued their polishing. "Just take a deep breath so your imagination doesn't get ahead of you. Tell yourself you can do it."

Nav couldn't stand it anymore. "Sounds like Kit could use a hand," he commented. "I could even offer her a little boost into the saddle—"

"Done!" Will yelled, dropping his rag and stepping back triumphantly.

Nav stopped polishing. "You can't possibly be done."

"Yeah, well, the less you talk, the more work gets done."

Nav clenched his teeth. A slob like Will couldn't possibly have beaten him and done a good job. "I'm going to check your work."

"Go for it," Will replied. "I'll be helping." He jerked his thumb behind him, indicating Kit.

He ran out, leaving Nav to examine his untidy pile of work rags and polish. "Pigsty." Then Nav got an idea and pulled out his mobile phone. . . .

Will quietly approached TK's stall. "Who can handle the wildest horse in here?" Rudy was asking his daughter. "You. That's rare. That's special. And remember, growing up, you spent nearly every weekend at the ranch with your mom and me."

"Yeah, and then I fell off. And I remembered that horses are high and weigh, like, a bazillion pounds."

That made Rudy chuckle. "Do you know how many times I've fallen off? Too many times to count."

"Not helping," Kit said, dismayed enough by the whole dilemma that she added, "Rudy," knowing it would annoy her dad. It was a childish thing to do, but the fact that her dad had fallen off a dozen horses just didn't make her feel any better.

Will made his move and entered the stall. "Hey, what if you rode something else?" he suggested.

"Like what, a train?" Kit asked. "Great idea."

"No, like something that's not a horse," said Will, "like a pony or something."

Josh was good at rugby. Though Covington stressed the equestrian arts and left little time for students to do much more than maintain their classes and ride, he'd made sure to squeeze enough time into his schedule for the rugby team as well. He was high-energy; he needed to keep moving. Then there was the matter of physique. He was determined to develop a six-pack. Girls liked six-packs, and he liked girls, so it only seemed logical.

He was heading for his room in Juniper Cottage after practice, thinking manly thoughts about six-packs, which then made him thirsty for a fizzy drink, when he stopped. Something nudged at the back of his mind.

He had just passed a bench. Something about it . . .

When he turned around to look again, he recognized the person sitting on it. Oh, she was wearing a disguise, of sorts — dark glasses, printed kerchief over her dark hair, a raincoat over her uniform even though the sky was clear. She made him think of the old movie star Grace Kelly, whose movies his mother loved to watch on DVD. But this wasn't Grace Kelly.

"You know, I don't know which celebrity you are, but hey, can I get your autograph?" He sat down next to her.

"Hey, Josh," Anya answered quietly.

"I thought you had, like, extreme chicken pox."

"My roommate really knows how to sell a story."
Anya took off her glasses, turned to face him, and
asked out of nowhere, "How do you get ready? When
you're going to a show?"

It took a minute for Josh to shift from rugby/fizzy
drinks/girls to horse show preparation. "Eat a lot of
carbs, sleep tons, burn pictures of my rivals in a midnight ceremony beneath the blood moon—"

Anya stood up. "Forget it."

Josh reached out and took her arm, gently pulling her back to the bench. "I have a tack box with
all the stuff that Whistler needs," he said seriously.
"And then I have my own bag, and I have a checklist
for that. So, you know, a day or two before, I go down
the list and make sure that everything's in there. My
mom helped me work out a system."

A system. Anya liked that idea. "I've never really
lived by myself before."

"None of us have," Josh said. "Except maybe Elaine.
I think she was born fully formed and, like, forty."

That made Anya laugh, but her next question
was accompanied by a pleading expression. "No, I
mean, like, I've always had . . . *help*." She stressed
the word, as though there was some meaning that she
hoped he'd catch on to.

He puzzled over what she'd meant by *help*. "Like, help with a capital *H*? Like servants?"

Anya tipped her head one way then the other, trying not to commit to an answer.

Josh had already suspected that Anya was not your run-of-the-mill student. Of course she had servants! "Like riding instructors and coaches? Cooks, personal chefs, personal shoppers—nannies?" He clearly enjoyed the idea and eagerly asked her, "Oh! Did you have one of those ladies who, like, handed you a towel after you washed your hands? Or one of those dudes who would taste the food and make sure, like, nothing was messed with?"

Josh could see relief flooding through Anya. She nodded. "Something like that."

"That is sweet!" He turned serious again. "Listen, Big A, it makes total sense that you had a tough time getting ready for the meet. It was like a first for you."

"But you think I could learn?"

All he could think was how cute she looked when she needed reassurance. "Yeah," he told her, and he meant it.

Kit entered the practice ring after Will. The only reason she was actually going to try this was because it was Will's idea. That didn't mean she was happy about it. Anything but.

"You promise she's not scary?" she asked.

"I promise," Will assured her. They crossed the grass, heading for a post where a saddled pony stood ready and waiting. "I give you—Mrs. Whiskers!"

Mrs. Whiskers's back swayed slightly, and her brown coat had a noticeable gray tinge to it. If there was such a thing as a sweet, old granny horse, Mrs. Whiskers was it. The pony flicked an ear as if in greeting but kept munching from a little pile of hay. Kit figured that if an alien rocket ship landed in the practice ring, Mrs. Whiskers would give it a glance and then go back to chewing.

"Okay, even I can agree to the fact that she looks pretty unscary," Kit admitted. "She's big, though."

"Well, TK's about sixteen hands," said Will. "She's barely twelve. She'll fit in your pocket."

Kit knew that the size of a horse was measured in hands, with one hand equaling four inches. The measurement was taken from the ground up to the horse's withers, which was the little ridge between their shoulder blades. That meant that TK, being sixteen hands high, measured sixty-four inches tall. Mrs. Whiskers, at twelve hands, measured a mere forty-eight inches tall. Kit could see right over her back.

"Plus, she's about a million years old, and she's had a million different riders," Will went on, trying to encourage Kit, "so she'll be fine. Do you want to go for it?"

This was it. The moment of truth.

A thrill of terror shot through Kit's innards, making her tremble. *I don't want to do this, I don't want to do this, I don't want to do this,* ran through her mind, along with *I have to do this, I have to do this, I have to do this.* She felt her body shrink into itself as if trying to hide right there in the open field. "I forget how to start."

Will grinned. "Left foot in the left stirrup, then you swing your right leg over the back of the saddle, and up you go."

"She's eating!" Kit blurted, pointing at Mrs. Whiskers as if Will might not have noticed all that loud nonstop chewing. "Is that okay? Maybe I should wait. Maybe *I* should eat!"

"Kit." Will sounded sympathetic, but he was also cutting her excuses short. She had to do this, and they both knew it.

"I'm still scared."

Will tried a different approach. "Do you know what I'm scared of? Snakes."

"You're just saying that."

"No, I'm not. Have you seen the way they move? They're like cut-off fingers that want to crawl all over you." He shivered. "I once jumped off a footbridge just 'cause someone made a hissing noise."

That was quite an admission coming from someone like Will. "I like snakes," Kit said. "Have you seen the video where the snake eats the entire porcupine?"

"No, no . . ." Will grimaced a bit in horror at the mere idea, but caught himself and focused on Kit. "Okay, quit stalling. C'mon, you can do it."

Kit tried to feel gung ho. "I can do it. I got this." She placed her left foot in the left stirrup, grabbed the reins and mane in her left hand, made a little hop—

And fainted.

Chapter 14

RECOVERY & REVENGE

K it awoke with a start. Had she been napping? It was broad daylight. Why was her bed so lumpy and cold? And why was Will staring at her? And her dad? And . . .

Oh.

She struggled to a sitting position with a moan. "Did I do it?" she asked weakly. Her head was spinning, and her stomach didn't feel so great, either. Thankfully, she didn't think she was going to hurl.

"So close," Will said to her. "Sooooo close."

With help from Will and her dad, Kit managed to stand. "You need a snack and a rest. Come on." Rudy wrapped an arm around her and pulled her close.

Kit leaned into him, gratefully letting him take her weight since her own stupid legs refused to do it.

"Feel like I'm four again," she grumbled. "Thanks anyway," she said over her shoulder as Rudy steered her toward Rose Cottage.

"That's all right," Will answered.

"I was talking to Mrs. Whiskers."

Kit didn't see Will's worried smile.

He led Mrs. Whiskers back to her stall, removed her tack, and gave her a light rubdown. Then he headed for Juniper Cottage. He was still determined to help Kit get on a horse, but in the wake of their recent disaster, what could he possibly do? It was time to lie back in bed, snarf some junk food, and do some serious thinking.

He never got the chance. The sight that greeted him when he opened his dorm room door shocked him so much that, at first, he thought he'd walked into the wrong room.

Someone had violated his personal space and done unspeakable things to it. His side of the room was . . . it was *clean*. It was *more* than clean. It looked like a magazine ad! It was tidy, organized, spotless!

Perfectly made bed, floor clear and hoovered, knick-knacks sorted, piles of laundry folded and put away—for goodness sake, someone had actually placed a ripe red *apple* on his neatly stacked schoolbooks!

It was like looking at the bedroom of his evil twin.

"Oh, gross," Will muttered, dropping his bag. "Where am I going to find clean socks? Where am I going to find *anything*?" His system was completely ruined!

He knew who to blame, of course. Nav. As revenge for his having won their tack-cleaning contest, Nav must have cleaned his side of the room, or rather, hired someone to do it. Nav would never clean such a mess himself. Well, there was only one way to respond, wasn't there?

Will snatched up Nav's spotless white cricket uniform.

Not long after, Will stood atop a damp grassy hill waiting for Nav. He had sent his roommate a mysterious text: "Trailhead Hill. 2:00. Be there."

Trailhead Hill wasn't very far from the main school building. It wasn't a very big hill, either. It only had a name because it was the starting point for one of the best riding trails on campus. But everyone knew where it was, and it was the perfect spot for Will to exact his revenge.

Nav arrived on time, expecting to witness some kind of prank. When he saw Will dressed in his cricket whites, he said in a bored voice, "Ha, ha, you're wearing my clothes. Okay." He did not expect what came next.

With a wild, "Woooo!" Will threw himself down the hill, deliberately rubbing his arms hard in the muddy grass and making sure to get as much dirt all over the cricket whites as possible. By the time he reached the bottom and leaped back to his feet, arms raised in victory, he was absolutely filthy.

Nav watched all this from the top of the hill, hands in his pockets, his face impassive. Then he sighed. "Barbarian," he said, and walked away.

Kit ate a snack as Rudy requested: a packet of trail mix, a banana, and a glass of milk. It made her feel slightly better, but only slightly. She decided to study the Covington Training Manual for a while. What she really wanted to do was talk to somebody about what had happened. She considered calling Charlie, but the thought of that just made her feel sad. Maintaining a close relationship from across the globe was proving to be more difficult than either of them had anticipated. Besides, Charlie was just getting to school for the day in Montana.

After twenty minutes or so, Anya skipped through the door carrying a load of fresh laundry.

"Where have you been?" Kit asked, relieved to see her.

"I was in the room of washing machines and drying machines!" Anya chirped happily.

Kit didn't notice Anya's happy demeanor. She just needed to talk. "My worst totally happened!" she blurted out.

"I've never done laundry before. It was exhilarating—wait, what?"

"I fainted," Kit told her miserably. "In front of Will. I tried to get on this pony, and she looked like a toy, but still . . ."

"Oh, no."

Kit used her hand to mime a tree falling down. "Timber! Right into the dirt." An awful thought came to her. "Do you think you drool when you faint?

Because if I drooled on Will, it's my turn to never leave this room."

"Definitely not," said Anya. "It probably just looked like you were resting your eyes."

Kit's chest tightened up. The world seemed to get dark. "I'll never ride," she whimpered. "I mean, Mrs. Whiskers was, like, this big!" She pinched her finger and thumb together.

Anya set her laundry down. "Okay, let's revamp," she said reasonably. "Best/Worst."

It was just what Kit needed to hear. Her chest loosened up. The world got a little brighter again. "Okay. Best is obvious. I climb up on TK, and it's wonderful, and we gallop through the fields with a rainbow coming out of his tail like some kind of unicorn magic."

That made Anya laugh. "Worst?"

Kit didn't even have to think about it. "I'm eighty-six, and I still live here, in this room, and I can't go anywhere because I haven't managed to ride—oh, and Elaine's granddaughter is shoving schedules in my face all day long, and you live in Italy—"

"Oooh, I love Italy!" Anya interrupted, then she caught herself. "Wait, let's start with the small things."

"Like?"

"Well, I needed to learn how to do my own laundry, and see?" She pulled a shirt from her pile and proudly held it up.

It was pink. It wasn't supposed to be pink. It *had* been white. Now it was pink. And small, very small, as in, small enough to fit a three-year-old child.

Kit tried to look sympathetic. "Wow, you decided to start with the *really* small things."

Anya threw down the shirt. "Oh, I'm a failure!" She flopped onto her bed and hid under the duvet.

"No, wait!" Kit moved over to the Anya bed lump. "You tried. Did you know how to use a washing machine at all before yesterday?"

"No," the bed lump admitted.

Kit pulled the duvet back. "Now you do! Sort of." She knew her next words would sound silly, but she meant them: "You're my hero." She paused. "And I'll teach you the cold cycle. And how to sort."

The offer made Anya's heart glow. Kit was proving to be one of the nicest people she'd ever met. There she was, shoulder-deep in her own misery, and she was trying to make Anya feel better. "But I wasn't *afraid* of washing machines," Anya pointed out, trying to turn the conversation back to Kit.

"As far as you know. Maybe you were attacked by one as a baby and just blocked it out."

"Unlikely."

Silence followed as both girls wallowed in their pity party. Then Kit declared, "We both need to keep going. Just like you said—small things. Baby steps."

Josh worked at the little tuckshop in the school's main building because he needed to ease his school fees in any way possible. But he quickly discovered that clerking at the tuckshop, the only retail outlet on the Covington campus, also put him in a most advantageous position.

For one thing, he'd met everyone in the school within the first two weeks of term. Nearly every student and teacher had come by to purchase something, whether it was a roll of breath mints, a mobile phone charger, or a pair of mittens. Second, working at the shop forced him to learn British terminology, which confused him to no end. For example, pants weren't pants: they were called *trousers*. Sweaters were called *jumpers*, though no jumping was involved. Undershirts were called *vests*, and a vest as he knew it was called a *waistcoat* (pronounced "westcut"). Raincoats were *macs*, short for *mackintoshes*, and no, those weren't computers. And *uni* didn't mean "uniform" but "university." Sometimes it made his head spin, but he was slowly getting it all straight.

Now Anya was standing at the service counter ordering a ton of clothing that, frankly, she should already have. "The show shirts are fifty-five dollars — er, pounds," he informed her, checking the price chart.

Anya nodded. "I'll take five."

"You mean, instead of the regular riding blouses?"

"As well as," she corrected him. "And the uniform blouses."

Josh totaled up her order. "That is, then, twenty shirts." He started to look up tax information but had to stop. "Wait, go back, go back — you're saying that she actually fainted?"

That was the other advantage of working at the tuckshop: gossip. Josh heard about everything, every little private tiff, student crush, and even teacher rivalry. His job had turned out to be the mother lode of gossip, a treasure trove of information that was sure to come in handy. And this latest tidbit was priceless—Kit had fainted while trying to mount the school pony, Mrs. Whiskers!

"Yeah," Anya told him, "but please don't make a big deal about it, okay? She's totally embarrassed. Kit's truly afraid . . . you know, like Will and his snake troubles."

Josh practically felt his ears grow bunny-big with this news. "What do you mean?" he asked, trying to sound only casually interested.

"Oh, he's so sweet," said Anya of Will. "Kit was all nervous, so he told her that he was afraid of snakes to make her feel better. And I think it worked."

"Huh." Josh tucked the tidbit in the corner of his mind labeled Juicy Personal Phobias to Exploit Later. Then it was back to Anya's order, which was a mystery in itself. "So for real," he said, "why are you getting all this stuff?"

Anya stood up straighter and adopted a determined expression. "Because I am *doing it.* I am making plans and getting organized and getting on top of things."

"But who needs twenty shirts? I didn't know you were such a princess."

Anya's determination turned to anger. "What did you call me?"

Josh gulped. "A princess?"

She scowled at him.

"What, is that some kind of gigantic insult here?" Good grief, yet another British term he didn't know!

"Don't call me that. It's rude!"

Josh was lost. "How?"

"Princesses are spoiled," Anya explained with distaste, "and they can't do anything for themselves. Why would anyone want to be friends with one?"

He made a wild stab in the dark. "They throw awesome parties and have private jets?"

"Yes, because of what they *have*, not who they *are*!" Anya forced herself back to calmness. "I have to go. Can you please put this on my account?" She hurried away.

"Wait, Anya!" Josh called. "Don't be mad!" He had meant it as a joke. What was with her, anyway?

Chapter 15

BABY STEPS AND
MORE REVENGE

In summary, current goals for Rose Cottage include earlier bedtimes, tidier corridors, and a long-term philanthropic plan. I intend to restore Rose Cottage to the top of the house standings."

"Best of luck with that."

Elaine did not appreciate Poppy's sarcastic remark. The prefects of all the girls' houses were having a meeting in Lady Covington's office, and Elaine was proud of what she'd just told the headmistress. She had plans for her house. She had goals. Poppy and the rest of the prefects were just messing around and wasting their opportunities, as far as she could see. That wouldn't get them into the best universities—that was for sure. "Yes, Poppy, I have been burdened with some challenging pupils this year," she said primly, "but I intend to rise to the challenge."

Lady Covington, seated behind her desk, seemed pleased with Elaine's report. "Thank you, Miss Whiltshire. Ladies, you're dismissed."

The girls rose and began to file out of the office.

"Miss Whiltshire," Lady Covington said before Elaine had moved a step, "would you mind?" She handed Elaine a letter.

Elaine smiled. The headmistress was handing her a handwritten letter! Usually that meant an invitation to tea! Was she finally being invited to tea with the headmistress personally? That was Elaine's dream, to finally reach such status that she was invited to tea! She accepted the letter with a trembling hand.

"Make sure that Miss Bridges gets that," Lady Covington instructed her. "It's rather important."

Elaine's smile threatened to melt, but she managed to freeze it in place. The second Lady Covington could no longer see her face, though, she snarled, and she kept snarling all the way out the door.

Back at the tuckshop, things were getting weirder for Josh. He was facing the back corner, prepping a clothes order, when the service bell went *clang*! He knew every sound the little bell made, and mostly it made a nice, soft *ting* that meant a customer was waiting for him. When the bell made a sharp *clang!* it meant that a customer in a rotten mood had given it a good whap.

He didn't much like *clang!* customers, but they came with the job.

He turned around to find a glowering Nav at the counter. "Cricket trousers," Nav said impatiently.

"Nav. Hey. Um, yes . . ." Josh decided it was safest to adopt a professional attitude. "Yes, those are a thing, and we do carry them." He turned away to pull a pair of neat white cricket trousers from the shelf. When he turned back around, a still-glowering Nav was holding up the trousers that needed to be replaced. They were covered in mud. "Where were you playing cricket, the dump?"

"I don't know what a dump is, exactly," said Nav. "This was Palmerston."

"Will did that to your pants?"

Nav's glower became darker, if that was possible. "They're called trousers. Pants are what you wear underneath."

Will gave up. "Just forget I asked. . . ."

"He did it because I had his half of our room cleaned," Nav explained in a more reasonable tone.

"Seriously?" Josh asked. "That's ungrateful!" And then Josh got an idea, one of those prime ideas that could only be acted upon in certain prime moments. This was one of those moments. "Listen, dude," he said, "I need to fill you in, okay? You are looking at one of the tidiest dudes you will ever meet. I mean, I alphabetize my shirts."

"How does that even—?"

"And do you know who my roommate is? Leo Ducasse. And do you know what we call him? He-Laine. I seriously need to move out, like, now. So, Palmerston can move into my room, and I'll move into yours. I travel light! I won't even bring stuff! I won't bring anything! I'll be way, *way* tidier—"

"It's definitely not that I want you to move in—"

"I bake! Did you know that? And I will throw these cricket trousers in for free—"

"I would genuinely prefer to pay for them, though that is a generous offer." Nav clenched his jaws. "And I will pay my roommate back for what he's done."

Josh wasn't about to let this opportunity go, not yet. He retrieved the latest piece of gossip from Juicy Personal Phobias to Exploit Later, only the *later* was *now*. "You know, I actually heard something rather interesting about him. . . ."

The Covington Training Manual was quite informative, as training manuals go, but it was dull. After having the heart-to-heart with Anya about taking baby steps, Kit had gone back to reading, but she just couldn't get her brain to engage. She decided to visit TK.

He'd been put in the outdoor practice arena to graze, since nobody was using it. When Kit arrived there, she found her dad leaning on the fence, one foot up on a low rail, his elbows propped on the top rail. He was watching TK. He was not smiling.

Kit came up beside him, and he immediately said, "You should still be in your room."

"I just got a little freaked out."

"Fainting is not *a little freaked out*. Fainting is your body saying, *Hey, stop it*. And if I have to choose between my daughter passing out and that jerk of a horse getting shipped out"—he pointed at TK—"it's *hasta la vista*, TK."

"Because family comes before a horse?" Kit asked.

"Because I still remember having to pick my kid up off the ground, take her to the hospital, and worry that she had a concussion, feeling like I was the worst father ever for letting her get anywhere near a horse."

Kit grasped her dad's arm and gave it an affectionate squeeze. "It wasn't your fault, Dad. It wasn't anybody's fault, not even Freckles, and that horse was a jerk." She expected her dad to say, "No, he wasn't," because Freckles had been a sweet horse really. She just couldn't help but think of him as a jerk ever since she'd fallen off him. "Falling happens," she said, once again recalling that day when she was eight and Freckles had carried her peacefully along Streamside Trail in the summer sun with the scent of lilies in bloom and the songbirds trilling in the brush. She never did find out what had spooked him, but Freckles had suddenly hopped to the left, startling her so badly that she fell right out of the saddle. "You don't even have to be on a horse to fall," she said, getting caught up in the memory. "It's just that he was . . . was running . . ." Oh, he had started to run, all right, galloping in a full panic. "And I couldn't get my foot out of the stirrup, and my head was bouncing along the ground, and his hooves were so close it felt like they were on my head. . . ." She could almost hear the drumming of those hooves again, loud, so horribly loud, the drums that had beaten so close and so loud that she'd thought her skull would explode.

Rudy glanced down at his daughter, a light of new understanding in his eyes. "So you're not afraid of getting on a horse," he said slowly, "and you're not afraid of riding a horse . . ."

His voice sounded strange. Kit looked up at him, wondering what he was getting at, and saw that light in his eyes. It seemed to shine right into her, and then—Kit's whole body tingled in sudden realization. The awful disjointed memories from six years ago shuffled around in her brain, finding a new order that suddenly made sense. "I'm afraid of being *dragged*," she breathed.

Rudy said nothing, letting her work through the next step.

Kit smiled, a big, wide toothy smile that spoke of new hope and courage. "Come on, TK!" she called to the horse in the arena. "We've got some baby steps to take together!"

Kit took TK to his stall and stayed inside with him, closing the door. Nobody else was in the stables. The peaceful quiet of the English country afternoon seeped through her, and she tried to project that feeling to TK.

"We're friends, right?" she asked him. "I don't want to hurt you, and you don't want to hurt me." She turned a bucket upside down and sat on it.

TK lowered his head to her level as if listening.

"So, between us, I'm still a little scared. So I'm going to face it head-on." Kit pulled her phone from her back pocket and tapped her timer app. "Thirty minutes of uninterrupted cuddle time. No matter what. Starting—" She programmed in thirty minutes and tapped the Start button. "Now." She set the phone aside and stood up. "Nobody ever got dragged during a cuddle," she informed TK, who huffed a hot breath at her as if to agree that the very idea was silly. Then he tried to nibble on her jacket.

Kit pulled her arm away, laughing. "Oh, I'm sorry, am I boring you?"

TK huffed again and nudged her.

His mellow mood gave Kit encouragement. "Okay. Let's just hug it out." She shifted closer so that his enormous horse head pressed against her chest.

They were practically eyeball to eyeball. "Good boy," she murmured, petting his cheek. "Good boy." She put her arms around his massive neck. TK stayed still as she continued closer, pressing the side of her face against his skin.

He was wonderfully warm, and she could hear him breathing inside, big inhalations of air whooshing up and down his windpipe like a bellows. The musky scent of his body calmed her. She hadn't let herself get this close to a horse in so many years! Yes, she had visited her dad's ranch on the weekends and had helped with chores in the stables, but only when the horses were out in the pasture.

Still, she had never lost her fascination for horses. Watching them gallop across open fields in playful groups, kicking up their heels and chasing each other, or playing with the big rubber balls that her mother bought for the babies in the spring. She had often laughed until she cried watching foals, all long skinny legs and no coordination, fumble around with the huge bouncy balls, trying to jump on them and falling off sideways, their short tails flapping in excitement at absolutely nothing but the fun of being alive.

Horses were amazing creatures, overflowing with personality if you took the time to notice. Freckles hadn't been a jerk at all. He had been a sweetheart, gentle enough to take care of an eight-year-old rider. It hadn't been his fault that instinct had told him to flee a perceived danger, whatever it had been that day. The simple shadow of a passing raven could spook a horse. It was just the way they were.

And TK wasn't a bad horse, either. As she hugged him, Kit felt as if he was trying to show her that he liked her and that he would be good to her if she was good to him. "Baby steps are nice," she murmured, closing her eyes and hugging him tight.

Will followed Josh down the steps of the main campus building. All academic classes were held within its many rooms, and they had just finished a math test up on the third floor. Josh seemed to be pleased with how he'd done, but Will couldn't help but worry. He wasn't good in math, and that last problem had been a killer. He hated dealing with numbers. All he wanted to do was work with horses. They made a lot more sense to him than numbers did. And people, for that matter.

He was so wrapped up in his thoughts that when the snake landed on his shoulder, it took him a good two seconds to recognize it—the sudden unexpected weight, the long, thin body draped over him, the diamond-shaped head pointing right at his face.

He screamed, jumping around and thrashing in terror, totally out of control. Nothing mattered but getting the thing off him. Every student in the lobby turned to stare as he danced in a mad circle, still screaming, until it dropped to the floor.

To his credit, it *was* a snake. And he had every right to hate snakes, especially if they fell on him from out of thin air. But a rubber snake? "Nav," he growled.

"No, haven't seen him," Josh said innocently, making a quick getaway.

"*Nav!*" Will hollered.

Nav waved cheerily from the stairs. "Was one of the First-Form girls just here? Because I swear I heard shrieking," he commented, sauntering down to lobby level and retrieving the rubber snake. "My ears are still ringing."

"Ha, ha!" Will thundered. "Are we even?"

"We're even." Nav draped the snake over his shoulders and stuck out his hand. "Gentlemen's agreement?"

Will reluctantly shook his hand. "You're lucky no one important was here."

Nav pulled his mobile out of his jacket pocket. "Oh! What do I have here?" He held it up to show a video playing—a video of Will battling the rubber snake. "Eighteen seconds of pure joy!" With a wild laugh, he darted away with his prize.

"No!" Will shouted, running after him. "No, Nav! Nav, don't you dare! Get back here!"

They disappeared down the hall amid the laughter of the other students.

Back in the stables, Elaine was stomping her way to TK's stall. Not only was she frustrated at not having been invited to tea with Lady Covington yet, but being ordered to deliver an invitation for exactly that to Kit Bridges was like rubbing salt in the wound.

She reached the stall and peered inside. Kit was there, as she'd been told, only the girl was asleep, right there in the hay. Elaine thought sleeping in a stall to treat a fear of horses was pretty stupid, but she also thought Kit Bridges was stupid, so there you go.

She placed the invitation on the door, leaning it against the bars so that Kit would see it when she woke up. Having completed her distasteful mission, she left.

It never occurred to her that TK would get involved. Elaine was hardly gone before he sniffed at the scented paper that Lady Covington always used. It smelled nice, like flowers. TK liked flowers.

He lipped the envelope into his mouth and ate it.

Chapter 16

TEA AND LANDMARKS

D ays passed, and Kit made progress with TK. She hadn't ridden him yet. She hadn't even tried to mount him. She was still working up the courage, but she knew the right time would come soon. She hoped it would. On a break from classes, she went to the stables.

Dressed in jeans, work shirt, work boots and a warm jacket, she maneuvered a wheelbarrow with a pitchfork over to TK's stall. "Hey, buddy," she greeted him. "Move over. Let's get this stall spick-and-span." She set up a little feedbag in the corner and tied him there so he would stay out of her way. He stuck his nose in the bag and started munching.

"You can use the indoor arena," came Rudy's voice from down the corridor, "just clean up your tack afterward. I don't want to be your stable maid."

"Roger that, Mr. B. Thank you," Josh's voice replied.

The two of them reached TK's stall as Kit started to clean. "Whoa," Josh said. "Is that what you're wearing to afternoon tea? That's risky."

Kit gave him a *you're nuts* face. "No, this is what I'm wearing to muck out TK's stall. Er, what tea?"

"Afternoon tea," Josh explained. "With Lady C? You're supposed to be there in, like, fifteen minutes. It's posted on her schedule."

Kit looked from Josh to her dad and back again. "It's the first I've heard of it!"

"You usually get an invitation from your house prefect," Josh told her.

"Elaine wouldn't . . . would she?"

Rudy held up a hand. "Now, that sounds like some serious conclusion jumping."

"I don't know. Girl warfare might be too complicated for your boy brain." Kit pulled a stray strand of alfalfa from her hair. "How do I do tea? What am I supposed to talk about with Lady C for an hour?

This is going to be a disaster!" She noticed more alfalfa in her hair and nervously pulled at it.

Rudy shook his head. "I've always been proud of how you don't overreact."

"I need a buffer," Kit decided. She looked straight at her dad. "I need a wingman! Rudy?"

"Oh, no, I can't," Rudy said quickly, injecting an *I'm very busy* tone to his voice. "Josh needs help getting Whistler back in order. Right, Josh?"

Josh smelled trouble and decided to help it along. "No, he's cool," he said to Rudy. He figured that if he kept his expression innocent, Rudy would never twig to the fact that he found this entire situation extremely amusing. As far as he could tell, Kit had her dad wrapped around her little finger.

"I'll see you outside Lady C's office in ten," Kit told her dad. "And change your boots. They're gross." She pushed her shovel into Josh's hands with an unspoken order to put the mucking gear away for her and left. Rudy glanced down at his grime-covered boots, sighed, and headed for his office to change.

Josh grinned. Oh, yeah, Kit was head of the Bridges family, all right.

Kit dressed back into her school uniform in under two minutes while reading from her mobile at the same time. "'Compliment the food. Compliment her dress.' Oh, thanks, tea etiquette website, I never would have thought of that!"

"Yes, you would have," said Anya, who was also getting dressed.

Kit faced the dorm room's big mirror, struggling with her hair. "Can you imagine? 'Oh, hello, Lady C. Do you mind changing? I can't look at that dreadful outfit for the next hour. And your cookies taste like cat food.'"

"Don't clink your spoon against your cup," Anya advised, grabbing up her books, "and don't pour the tea unless you're invited. It's a real honor to be asked."

"Thanks for being truly helpful."

"You have to be at Lady Covington's in seven minutes and three seconds!"

Kit studied herself in the mirror. She didn't look half bad, for someone dressed in a boring uniform. At least she'd gotten control over her alfalfa hair. After straightening her jacket, she turned to find Anya struggling to carry too much stuff. "That's a lot of books."

"I have to ace my architecture project, especially after I fluffed the big event," said Anya. "I just want to stay on top of things."

"You're paired with Nav, right? He seems like a smarty-pants."

Anya set her books back down and rooted around in her jewelry box. She held up a pair of earrings. "Do you think these earrings say *hardworking and intelligent?*"

"I don't know what you're so worried about. You're going to do great."

"Thank you. And you know, Kit, you can use anything from my wardrobe."

"Really?"

"Yeah. I'd really like that. Good luck! Got to dash! Bye!"

Kit glanced at the time on her phone. "Right. Five minutes and forty-eight seconds. Just enough time for a finishing touch." She opened Anya's wardrobe and gasped. She'd never peeked in there before and had no idea that it was a doorway to haute couture. "Oh," she murmured. "Hello there!"

Anya arrived in the student lounge, hunched over by the weight of all the books she was carrying. When Nav saw her dilemma, he jumped up, ever the gentleman. "Let me help you, Anya." He took her books and put them on the table, which allowed her to slip her tote off her shoulders and hang it on the back of a chair.

"Thanks," she said brightly. She couldn't wait to begin. Nav was a good student and would no doubt be a great project partner, and she fully intended to wow him with her own brilliance. Between the two of them, she was sure to ace this! Good grades were her only hope in winning back Lady Covington's faith in her.

"So," said Nav, "we need to choose a British landmark on which to base our drawing. There's Big Ben—"

Anya cut him off, excitedly pulling a folder from under her book pile. She had already considered Big Ben, which was one of the most well-known landmarks in London. The entire structure was actually the Houses of Parliament and Elizabeth Tower, while the name Big Ben technically referred only to the enormous bell in the clock tower. But most people just called the entire structure Big Ben.

Anya knew it was a very significant landmark, but she wanted to really stand out with this project. "I did some research," she proudly stated, "and these are my thoughts. I've highlighted the ones of interest." She stopped, noting how Nav's mouth had dropped open in shock at all the material she had assembled. Had she gone too far? It was so hard to tell. She decided to let him take the lead. "Or Big Ben," she said, gently pulling the folder back out of his hands. "And just never mind that stuff."

"Excellent," said Nav. "I'll get started on my half after lunch." He prepared to leave.

"Wait!" Anya had one more idea. "Anyone can draw Big Ben. Why don't we build a scale model? I mean, we could really make an impression with this project."

Nav's eyes lit up. "That's an inspired idea! And I know exactly what to do to take it to the next level of genius!" He bent over his papers and began to scribble notes while Anya opened their textbook.

Kit dashed into the main building, determined to get to Lady Covington's office on time. She was cutting it close, but it had taken her a few minutes to choose a finishing touch for her outfit from the amazing choices in Anya's wardrobe. She'd never been to an English tea, though she'd seen them on TV shows. Characters on TV always dressed up for tea, so she'd chosen a little pink froufrou hat to add some spice to her otherwise bland uniform.

She turned a corner to find Elaine flipping through a handful of printed posters. The unexpected sight of the girl angered Kit. She glanced at her mobile. "Four minutes, six seconds." She had enough time. "Quick question," she said loudly at Elaine. "Who is it that is responsible for delivering invitations from Lady C?"

Elaine took her sweet time acknowledging the question. When she finally opened her mouth to answer, though, she said, "Oh!" Her eyes scanned Kit from head to toe then back up to her head. "I see you're ready."

"Yeah," said Kit, "I didn't get an invitation until just now. So how does the system work exactly?"

Elaine focused back on her posters. "I delivered yours promptly after instruction. I left it in your donkey's stall."

"Well, I never got it."

"Hm, interesting." Elaine pretended to think it over. "Oh, wait. No. It's not!"

Kit wanted to kick herself. How could she have expected any other answer from someone like Elaine? "Thanks a lot." She resumed her way down the hall.

"Oh, love the fascinator, by the way," Elaine added with a syrupy smile. "Dead-on for teatime."

Is that what this kind of hat is called? A fascinator? Kit thought. She could probably trust Elaine to know such a thing, but the fact that Elaine complimented her on it? *Don't try to figure it out,* she advised herself.

When she reached Lady Covington's office, her dad was already there, seated and looking incredibly uncomfortable. "Hello!" Kit hurried over to the empty chair and sat. "I thought I was on time! Ish."

Lady Covington stared at her with a strange expression, then smiled. "One might consider arriving ahead of schedule, but perhaps another day." Her smile actually got bigger. "And your father has decided to join us for tea."

"Oh, yeah." Kit glanced at her dad, who grimaced back at her. She wished he could fake his way through awkward social situations, but he wasn't that kind of guy. If he was nervous, everyone within a mile knew it. "I invited him. Is that bad?"

"Worse things have occurred . . . in a general sense," Lady Covington replied, "but perhaps it's good he's here. We have much to discuss. Would you care to pour the tea, Mr. Bridges?"

"Oh, I'm not much of a tea drinker," Rudy said, planting a forced smile on his lips. "I'm more of a coffee man."

Lady Covington turned to pick up a beautiful three-tiered serving tray filled with delicate tea cakes and pastries, so Kit took the opportunity to kick her dad in the shin for saying something so lame. Clueless, Rudy glared back at her while keeping the fake smile. If Kit weren't feeling so anxious, she would have laughed out loud.

Instead she watched the headmistress place the tray on the table next to an ornate tea set. Lady Covington poured the tea herself, handing cups to Kit and Rudy whether they wanted them or not, then poured for herself. Kit tried to memorize every move she made in case this occasion were ever to happen again, but seeing as it had started off so badly, she doubted that it would. Still, one could never predict the future, so she attempted to salvage the situation. "Isn't this a lovely spread, Dad?" she said, trying to use ESP to tell him, *Compliment her pearls! Compliment the tea! Say something!*

He did: "Oh, yeah. And that chocolate cake looks almost as good as your mom's mud pie."

Kit considered crawling under the couch.

"Mud pie?" Lady Covington said with interest. "That's a delicacy I'm not familiar with."

"It's what my mom used to call a chocolate pie," Kit stammered. "It was awesome, but I'm sure that this cake is a bit better." To prove it, she grabbed a piece from the tray and shoved it into her mouth whole. "Mmm!" she hummed, feeling like a squirrel with a face full of nuts.

"Let us move on to a more pressing matter," Lady Covington suggested. "It has come to my attention that you have yet to ride TK. That is not acceptable."

Kit's eyes widened. She dearly wished she'd taken a small bite of the cake instead of panicking and shoving the whole thing in. She couldn't talk!

Lady Covington turned to Rudy. "Mr. Bridges, was I a fool to assume that you would champion your daughter onto a horse?"

"My daughter will ride when she's ready," Rudy stated.

Kit knew that tone of voice. Her dad was going into serious Parental Mode. *Nooooo!* she thought, frantically sucking on the chocolate blob in her mouth, trying to shrink it down to a chewable size so she could stop this train before it wrecked.

Lady Covington gave Rudy the patient stare of a queen to her servant. "No," she stated simply. "We will begin with some cantering and some small jumps, then we'll move on to something a little more challenging."

Rudy sat up straighter. "Not until she says she's ready, and even then, your schedule is unreasonable."

"It is perfectly reasonable," the headmistress insisted, "and it is what will happen."

Kit furiously sucked on the chocolate blob.

Rudy set down his tea. "You can undermine me as an employee. I can take it. But you will not undermine me as a father. I'll be the one who decides when Kit is ready for the arena."

"Every pupil must take part in horse-related activities. That is the rule. There are no exceptions."

"I'm not going to sit here and talk to someone who refuses to listen, especially when it's about my own kid." Rudy got up, threw a very plain glare at Lady Covington, said, "Thanks for the hospitality," and left the room.

Kit finally managed to speak. "Did you make this yourself?" She innocently gestured to the cakes still on the serving tray.

"No." Lady Covington's smile wasn't genuine, but Kit knew she was lucky to get any smile at all. "I was very serious about TK. He can only remain here on the guarantee that you will ride him. If you're not ready by our next scheduled meeting, he will be in a horse trailer on his way to auction faster than you can say mud . . . chocolate"—she nodded at the serving tray irritably—"pie. Are we clear?"

"Absolutely," said Kit. She made one final attempt to salvage the situation. "And thank you for the tea. It was . . . delightful?"

"You may go."

Kit stormed up to her father, who was out by the practice ring, leaning on the fence. "You escaped," he said in sarcastic relief. "I thought that dragon lady might have eaten you."

"How could you speak to her like that?" Kit exploded. "Now she's really going to have it in for me and TK!"

"Her schedule is nuts, kid. I'm not going to let her dictate your life, not when she's talking nonsense."

Kit didn't want to hear it. She was tired of adults messing around with her life. "I'll do whatever I have to to keep my horse, even if it means keeping to her schedule!"

"But you haven't even sat in a saddle properly yet," Rudy pointed out, trying to be reasonable. "She had you cantering and jumping next week!"

"If it means that we stay together, then TK and I will do it—whether you believe in us or not!" Kit folded her arms and gave her dad the same glare that he had given Lady Covington only minutes before. It was the Bridges Glare, and it meant only one thing: trouble.

Chapter 17

USING YOUR RESOURCES

S tudy period in the lounge found at least a dozen students tapping away on laptops or sitting with their heads in textbooks.

Not Josh. He was pondering a photo of the building he was going to draw for his architecture project: 30 St. Mary Axe, a famous skyscraper in the London financial district. It had been completed in 2003 and was architecturally unique in the London skyline because it looked like a giant pickle. It was, in fact, commonly known as the Gherkin. Josh considered a giant pickle building too good to pass up, but he couldn't figure out how to draw it. Since his project partner wasn't available, he turned to the student studying at the nearest desk. "Yo, slacker."

Elaine looked up.

"Can I ask some advice? How am I supposed to draw a round building on a flat piece of paper?"

Elaine rolled her eyes. "Try asking your partner. I'm busy." Her curiosity got the better of her. "Why do you ask, anyway? What building are you drawing?"

"The Gherkin!" Josh held up the photo. "Coolest building in London, yeah?"

"That's hardly a classic English design," Elaine stated in a superior tone.

Josh frowned. "It totally is."

Elaine held up her photo. "Peaches and I chose a building of historical significance."

A loud sarcastic snoring sound came from the couch where Will was lying, reading a magazine with his headphones on.

Elaine lowered her photo, looking almost stricken. "What does that mean?"

"Buckingham Palace?" Will said, pulling his headphones off. "It's been done over and over."

"It's better than drawing a pickle. Did you know that's what he's doing?" Elaine indicated Josh.

Will leaned forward on the edge of the couch. "Why do you care?"

"Because he's not taking it seriously, and the rest of us care. He's predictable, and he's lowering the bar for us all."

Will gave her a strange look. "It was my idea. Josh is my partner."

"Oh." Elaine's face tried on several odd expressions before settling into what looked like cosmic enlightenment. "Well, I mean, I suppose it could work. For you. It *is* interesting."

Josh stared at her, fascinated. He'd never seen Elaine remotely concerned with what other students did regarding their schoolwork, yet here she was, debating it with Will, of all people.

"Yeah," Will was saying, "not to mention innovative. Modern, yeah? Fresh?"

"Yeah." Elaine fiddled with her hair. "I . . . I wonder if I should reconsider *my* project. What do you think?"

Now Josh was just plain shocked. Elaine suddenly doubted her choice of subject because Will Palmerston made a comment? Elaine never let anybody change her mind. She usually got all superior and made the other person feel like dirt. "If this wasn't happening right in front of my eyes, I'd never believe it," he murmured.

"I didn't ask your opinion," Elaine snapped at him, then gave Will a sappy smile as she closed her laptop and gathered her books. "I'll keep you posted," she said to him, and left.

"Once," Josh mused, "just once, I want to be able to knock her off her game like that. I mean, did you hear her? She's like, *Oh, he's not taking this seriously. He's too predictable.*"

Will grinned. "Yeah. You just need to know what makes her tick." His grin faded. "Oh, and *no.*"

"To what?"

"The building." Will jerked his head at the Gherkin photo.

"But, dude, it looks like a giant pickle!"

"Mate, we're doing Saint Paul's." Will resettled his headphones and went back to reading his magazine.

Josh stared at the Gherkin photo and sighed.

Anya had been eager to hear Nav's idea for their architecture project, but she never dreamed it would be so—professional. Literally! He had used his family connections to fly a professional architect named Nina in from London!

Now she, Nina, and Nav were out on the school grounds. They'd picked a spot on the grass that would be the perfect place to work.

"We'd like you to help us build the model," Nav told Nina, indicating the spot. Nina nodded and scribbled notes into a little notepad.

Anya couldn't stop her imagination from riding the idea train. "*Is* that what we'd like?" she asked Nav. "Is that *all* we'd like?"

"What are you saying?" Nav asked. "Nina is one of the most accomplished architects in Britain."

"Let's *improve* Big Ben!"

Nina scribbled notes as Nav considered the idea. "Build a better version . . ."

"Exactly!" said Anya. "And do you know what I've always thought Big Ben needed? A rooftop pool!"

Nav gazed into space, smiling. "*Everything* needs a rooftop pool."

Nina scribbled more notes.

By the time they were done, Nina's little notebook was crammed with scribbling, and she had drawn up a professional set of plans. Anya and Nav thanked her and ran to the student lounge to show them off.

To their delight, Josh and Will were in the lounge working on their project.

"Here's the rooftop pool," Anya explained to them, pointing at the plans for their new and improved Big Ben. "And Nav has an amazing idea for the clockface."

"Every hour," Nav declared, "it lights up in a different color."

Josh was impressed. "Oh, man! Elaine is going to freak when she sees how next-level you guys went with this."

Will frowned at him. "Hey, there's nothing wrong with Saint Paul's Cathedral."

"Or there *won't* be if you just let me add the chairlift, dude," said Josh. "A half-pipe for snowboarding, right off the steeple? Come on, please?"

Kit marched into the room. By now her fascinator had slid down so that it looked more like a frilly pink crustacean clinging to the side of her head. "Well, today was a total disaster!" she cried, the fascinator jiggling as she spoke. "I never should have taken my dad with me! He had a huge fight with Lady C, and now I'm supposed to be cantering right this minute and—" She paused as the colorful plans in

Anya's hand caught her eye. "What did you guys do to Big Ben?"

"We added a rooftop pool," Nav explained as if such a thing should have been done a hundred years ago.

"And a helicopter pad!" Anya chirped with excitement.

Nav added, "Because last time I tried to do some sightseeing, it was such a nightmare trying to land."

"Yeah, well, who hasn't been *there*?" Will quipped from the back table.

"Kit," said Anya, "is that what you wore to afternoon tea?" She pointed at the drooping fascinator.

"Yeah," Kit answered, suddenly noting how they were all looking at her funny. "Why?"

"Well, it's feathery . . ." Will began. "And lacy. And . . . and pink, which is . . . which is cool."

"Cool," Josh repeated, his eyes twinkling with mirth.

Kit was not in the mood for teasing. They were teasing her, weren't they? She couldn't tell, and that made it even worse. "You guys!" she snapped, just wanting them to stop.

Josh decided to show mercy and took it upon himself to tell poor Kit the truth. Though, being who he was, he couldn't do it nicely. "Josh Luders here, Fashion Coroner," he said, straightening his tie and trying to sound official. "Time of death?" He let the moment build, then called out, "The moment that thing went on your head!"

Everyone burst out laughing. It was mean to tease Kit, but they couldn't hold it back anymore. She looked too goofy to ignore.

"Why can't I get any of this British stuff right?" Kit wailed.

Anya rushed over to her roommate. "On the bright side, it probably distracted Lady C from how wonky your tie is." She straightened said tie.

That made Kit deflate even more. "I would have been better off showing up with hay all over me!"

"Did Elaine not tell you about the invitation?" asked Josh. "If you'd gotten the invite in time, you probably would have been able to make the right hat choice. I say *probably* because"—he waved his hand in her direction—"you might still have gone with *that*."

Will busted up laughing again.

"Elaine told me she delivered it," Kit said grimly, "and she told me I looked great on my way to Lady C's."

"She could have stopped this?" Anya said. "That's some seriously bad karma she's brought on herself."

Josh nodded in agreement. "What goes around comes around."

Even Will stopped smiling at the thought of what Elaine had done. Or more important, not done.

Kit let Anya gently remove the fascinator, then she headed off to her room.

Anya and Nav returned to the building spot they had chosen outside for their model. Nav stepped back and forth, a hand to his ear. "Ooooooooo, eeeeeeeee, ooooooooo," he intoned with intense concentration. "Yup! This, acoustically speaking, is the perfect space for the musical water feature."

Anya smiled at him. She was so impressed by all the technical things he knew. She was starting to think he was a genius. "Will you describe the glass floor to the class?" she asked him. "You do it so well."

Before he could answer, Sally arrived, looking very put out. "Nav, why on earth was your family helicopter on school property?"

Rudy marched up right behind her. "Can someone explain why there's chalk on the field? My field?"

Anya looked back and forth between the two adults. "It's our architecture project. We decided to build a new and improved Big Ben!" She held up Nina's plans.

Indicating the plans, Nav added, "And naturally, we flew in the best architect we could find."

Sally took one look at the plans and shook her head. "Aside from Mr. Bridges needing the field for horse riding, having an architect design your model is *cheating*."

Both Anya and Nav reacted to that word with alarm. Cheating? They had only been doing their best!

"You need to complete the project by your deadline," Sally went on, "and without a professional doing the work for you."

What would have been obvious to most students in the world slowly came into focus for Anya—and, judging from the look on his face, for Nav as well. She realized that *doing your best* meant doing your *personal* best, not doing your best given your resources, of which both she and Nav had plenty. It kind of made sense, although it had at first made more sense to them to use their vast resources to do the best job.

But maybe that wasn't the point. Maybe their architecture project was supposed to teach them more than just how to build a building. Maybe it was really a way to help them build *themselves* by gaining self-confidence and maybe even a sense of personal responsibility.

"We're sorry, Miss Warrington," Nav said, and Anya could tell that he meant it. She could also tell that he didn't like being lectured but was beginning to understand.

Anya nodded her apology as well. After all, wasn't she here to learn how to do things by herself? This project could help her learn to do exactly that!

"No need to apologize," Sally told them both. "Just go and get started. On your own."

Anya and Nav nodded obediently, then headed back to the student lounge to plan anew.

That left Sally and Rudy still standing in the field. "You have to admire their ability to think outside the box—and the building," Sally said with a chuckle. She knew she should probably have been more strict with the two students, but having come from a wealthy family herself, she knew how difficult it was for some rich children to learn not to rely on wealth for all the answers in life.

Rudy made a *harrumph* sound. "Everybody in this school needs to be brought back down to earth." He was crabby, more crabby than Sally had ever seen him. Something more was weighing heavily on him.

"Would you like to talk about what's really bothering you, Mr. Bridges?"

Rudy hemmed and hawed and finally confessed, "I had a throw-down with Lady C."

"Again?" Sally asked. It seemed like the two of them were *throwing down* a lot lately.

"And then Kit stopped talking to me because I wasn't doing whatever Lady Covington wanted," Rudy continued.

Sally tried to hide a smile. "Kit got mad at you because you weren't doing what you were told? Curious."

"After her riding accident, I pressured her to get back on, and it backfired," Rudy explained. "I don't want to blow it again, certainly not to please that dragon lady."

Sally laughed inwardly. Personally, she liked Lady Covington. A lot. The woman was nicer and a lot more human than most people believed. From the outside, Lady Covington was strict, demanding, and unforgiving, but what most people forgot was that she had to run a school full of privileged students, kids who needed a very firm hand so they didn't grow up to be spoiled, uncaring adults. It was a challenging job, but Lady Covington was very good at it. She had to be a bit harsh to get the job done right.

Sally had experienced this firsthand, having attended Covington many years ago. The school had changed her life, and all for the better. Someone like Rudy, who seemed to be naturally practical and responsible and humble and caring, had a hard time understanding why everybody didn't toe that line. And now that his own daughter was under Lady Covington's watch, he was taking some of Kit's lessons personally.

Sally could relate to that. She often felt bad when, as a teacher, she had to reprimand a student. And sometimes when Lady Covington came down hard on a student, Sally herself cringed, remembering what it felt like to be on the receiving end. Rudy was just trying to protect his daughter while also settling into a new job, a new country, and a school full of new rules and regulation and traditions. None of this was easy for him, and Sally wanted to help.

"Girls can be complicated creatures," she said. "One minute they need you, the next they act like you're the biggest embarrassment ever. My advice . . ." She thought hard for a way to make it clear to him. "Pretend she's one of your horses," she suggested. "Give her space, and she'll gallop off and do her own thing, but"—Sally looked into Rudy's eyes—"she'll come back when she's ready."

Rudy just shrugged, which amused her. Was this typical cowboy behavior? Was Rudy Bridges a typical cowboy? She would never know for sure, but she hoped so. The British had a very romantic idea of what American cowboys were like, and so far, Rudy fit that idea pretty well.

Back in the student lounge, Anya and Nav pondered their dilemma. How could they build a model of

Big Ben in time yet stay true to their extraordinary plans?

"We could use boxes?" Nav wondered out loud. "Sugar cubes?" He thought some more. "Papier-mâché!"

"It won't dry in time," Anya said, "and we'll never make the deadline. And then we'll get expelled, and we won't be allowed near Covington again!"

At the table behind them, Josh's voice floated over: "It's so cool that we're done." Slurping noises accompanied this pronouncement.

Anya glanced over her shoulder, saw what was going on, and jumped to her feet. "What are those?" she demanded of Josh and Will.

The boys were leaning back in their chairs eating something off sticks. "Ice lollies," they said at the same time.

Anya's smile could have lit up a stadium. She grabbed the near-finished ice lollies and held them up. "I've got it!"

"Get your own!" Josh and Will said, again at the same time. They grabbed for their treats, but Anya held them out of reach.

"This is an emergency," she said. "Nav, fetch the glue gun. We are getting an A plus if it takes us all night!"

Nav took one look at the ice lollies—specifically, the sticks—and realized Anya's plan. He grinned and ran off to get supplies.

Chapter 18

MODEL BEHAVIOR

Elaine began the next day by putting up more posters in the main building hallways before classes. She was in charge of several aspects of the school's upcoming Guy Fawkes celebration, and she wanted all the students to be well aware of that fact and ready to help. The last person she wanted to see was Peaches who, though a loyal friend, could be terribly annoying at times.

Peaches scurried up to her, excited about something. Everything excited Peaches. She was a very excitable girl.

"Personal space, please, Peaches," Elaine told her. She was so tired of having to remind Peaches of these things.

"Sorry, Elaine," Peaches said in her cute, high-pitched voice. "It's just—"

"It's just I'm extremely busy right now, so . . ." Elaine let her sentence trail away, expecting Peaches to make an exit.

Instead of leaving, Peaches took one deliberate step back and blurted out, "I was told that you're wanted in Lady C's office for afternoon tea immediately!"

Elaine almost dropped her posters. How could this have happened? She hadn't heard a thing about it! "Immediately?" she breathed, stunned.

"Yes!" said Peaches. "It's such an honor, isn't it? I've dreamed of going someday, too. Ooh-ooh, can I come?" she pleaded. "I promise not to—"

But Elaine was already striding off.

Kit was having a heart-to-heart talk with TK in his stall.

"All right, everything is going to be fine," she told him, running her fingers through his silky black forelock. "We just have to follow this schedule to a T, because there is no way I am letting them take you away from me." She skimmed over her printout of Lady Covington's riding schedule. "Um . . . is she joking? She wants us to be jumping oxers in a *week*?"

TK communicated his opinion by ripping off part of the schedule and eating it.

"Dude!" Kit scolded him and moved the paper out of his reach. "That's okay," she said, referring to the schedule again. "We can do this. You know, it's possible . . . we could do it . . . in this century . . ."

TK bit off another part of the schedule and ate it.

"Probably." Kit gave up. It was hopeless. No matter how much she might want to honor the schedule, she couldn't, and she knew it. She let TK lip the rest of the paper from her hands. "You know what? Go ahead. Eat it. Get rid of it! It's a goner!" She stroked TK's nose as he chomped away. "Oh, boy, you're hungry. I'll go get you some hay."

As she left the stall, something caught her eye. At first she thought she was seeing scraps of the schedule that had dropped into TK's bedding, but that wasn't it—she could make out handwritten words. She picked up the scraps and examined them. "You ate my invitation?" she cried.

TK innocently gazed at her.

"Dude, I just yelled at Elaine!" Kit shut her eyes, knowing what she had to do now. "Oh, this is *so* not going to be good."

Elaine knocked on Lady Covington's office door, not too loudly but not too softly, either. She judged it to be just right: loud enough to hear, but reserved enough to be polite. When the headmistress opened the door, Elaine said, "Good afternoon, Lady Covington." She stepped in, immediately searching for something to compliment. "Oh my, are those new curtains?"

"Yes," came the headmistress's hesitant reply. "Should I have consulted you before purchasing them?"

"Oh, gosh, no! They're lovely. I love the fabric." Elaine took a seat on a cushy chair. "I just want to say thank you for inviting me. I truly appreciate it."

Lady Covington gave Elaine an odd look. "Actually—"

"I've waited so long for this opportunity, and I do love tea." Elaine glanced gleefully at the serving table, crowded with several three-tiered trays filled with goodies. "And cake."

A moment passed before Lady Covington responded. "Oh?"

Sally entered and said to her boss, "The gentlemen from the board are—oh! Elaine." She paused. "Uh, did I miss you from the schedule?"

Something clicked in Elaine's mind: Lady Covington's unusual expression, Sally's surprise, the strangely awkward conversation . . . She glanced again at the serving table, at how many trays and cups were set out, at how two people couldn't possibly warrant such an elaborate feast.

"Elaine," said Lady Covington, "I'm a bit confused as to the purpose of your interruption."

The puzzle came together. Elaine's heart dropped somewhere down around her ankles. "Um." She jumped up, realizing that she hadn't been invited after all. This was somebody's idea of a prank! Rage bubbled up within her, but she fought it down. First she had to remove herself from this horrible situation. Only then could she seek revenge. "Um. Yes. Absolutely. I won't keep you. Straight to the point, um . . . I would like to . . ." She combed her brain for something, anything to say—"to take on the role of . . . of tea and cake coordinator at next year's annual spring bake sale!"

Ever so slightly, Lady Covington's eyebrows lifted. "Because you love tea," she said slowly. "And cake."

"Exactly!" Elaine tried desperately to give the impression that this request was super important to her. In a way it was, because the moment she was free, someone was going to suffer.

Lady Covington was still groping to make sense of the conversation. "This couldn't wait until spring?"

"I like to be—" Elaine gulped. She liked to be what? What? *What?* "Forward thinking!"

"Indeed."

"Excellent! Well—" Elaine pointed at the door. "I'll be on my way. Thank you for seeing me." She left the room as quickly as possible, trying to maintain what little dignity she had left.

Oh, someone was going to suffer, all right, and she knew exactly who it was going to be.

Kit couldn't help but feel silly. Here she was, going from building to building, from room to room, trying to find the last person on earth she should ever want to find: Elaine Whiltshire. The irritating girl wasn't in her dorm room or any of the study rooms, and she didn't have class at the moment. Where in the world was she?

Kit tried the student lounge next. "Have you guys seen Elaine?" she asked Anya and Nav before she noticed that both of them were in a stupor, slumped at their table with glazed eyes. Then she saw why. "Whoa! What is this?"

Anya moaned her way back to life. "Our project," she said, pointing to it. "Big Ben." Her arm flopped back to the table. "So tired . . ."

"It's amazing!" Kit said, and it really was. Anya and Nav had built a lolly-stick model of Big Ben, and it was perfect. Kit wasn't entirely sure that Big Ben had a pool on the roof or a helicopter pad, but it looked incredible nonetheless.

"It took us all night," said Nav, his words slurring a bit.

Will and Josh came over to take a look. "And exactly how many Popsicles did you need to eat?" Josh asked.

While Will laughed at the idea of them forced to eat mountains of frozen ice lollies, Anya whimpered, "I never want to touch one again."

Kit pulled out her phone. "Do you want me to take a photo?" She angled up a nice shot of the model with an exhausted but smiling Anya and Nav behind it. Will and Josh horned in, too, leaning down into the shot with dopey grins on their faces. Kit snapped the photo. "So have you guys seen Elaine?" she asked them again, pocketing her phone.

"Maybe. Today?" Anya looked to Nav for confirmation, but Nav didn't look so sure.

"It was yesterday," he said tiredly.

"Really?" Anya shrugged at Kit. "I've lost track of time."

"That was the most childish prank in the history of Covington!" came Elaine's voice as she stormed into the lounge, her eyes blazing in fury. She directed that fury right at Kit.

Kit pointed at herself. "Are you talking to me? Because I have no idea—"

"Don't deny it! You set me up to look stupid in front of Lady C!"

"What?" Kit cried. "I was looking for you so I could apologize, actually. TK ate my invitation. I just found out."

Elaine was too busy snarling to listen to facts. "From the second you showed up, I knew you weren't fit to be one of us!" she shouted. "Same goes for your horse!"

That hit a nerve. "I have no idea what you're talking about! And at least TK isn't some kind of prissy diva horse like Thunder!"

Everyone in the lounge was watching now as the two girls verbally tore each other apart.

"I'll have you know that Thunder has won more ribbons at this school than any other horse!" Elaine said.

"Because you bullied him into it!" Kit shot back. "You're not as perfect as you think you are! I bet Thunder doesn't even like you!"

Will and Josh, who had been visibly enjoying the show, gasped at Kit's words. Kit herself was a bit shocked at what she'd said, even though Thunder *was* a prissy horse. Elaine did work him hard. Everybody knew it, but no one else was going to say it to Elaine's face.

The childish insult stung. "How *dare* you!" Elaine shrieked. She grabbed the closest object—a cup full of unused lolly-sticks—and threw it at Kit.

Kit didn't have enough time to figure out what the projectile was. She instinctively ducked, afraid that it might be something heavy. She threw an arm to one side, striking Big Ben. The model crashed to the floor in pieces.

"Katherine Bridges and Elaine Whiltshire!"

Everybody froze. Of all the voices they didn't expect to hear—of all possible people to have seen this very un-Covington-ish argument—Lady Covington was last on the list.

"My office!" Lady Covington continued, standing in the lounge doorway and radiating absolute rage. *"Now!"*

Chapter 19

PRIDE & PREJUDICES

Anya and Nav were upset, to say the least. All their hard work, smashed! They gathered up the pieces of their ruined Big Ben, placed them in a box, and trudged to Juniper Cottage.

Will and Josh were also heading to Juniper, but they walked ahead of Anya and Nav. "So as it turns out, Elaine wasn't even invited," Will informed Josh as they walked. "So she thinks that Kit set her up, but Kit—"

"Kit didn't do it," Josh said, and giggled.

Will looked at him. "How do you know?"

Josh remained silent, letting the sneaky grin on his face say it all.

"You did it?" said Will. "You sent Elaine walking into Lady C's office like she owned the place?"

Josh shrugged with mock humility. "I like to snowboard and call people dude, right? I don't have a fancy accent or anything, but that doesn't mean I'm a moron. Or *predictable*. And I'm definitely not *lowering the bar* for anybody."

Will remembered those words, the words Elaine had used to insult Josh earlier. Josh had gotten revenge, all right. "I can't believe you did that. That is gold! And gutsy."

Josh basked in the compliment, yet he still said, "I should probably apologize."

Will nodded. "Yeah, you really don't want to be on the bad side of Elaine. You'd better have a good plan for that."

They bumped fists. "Wish me luck," said Josh.

Behind them, Anya and Nav walked along carrying their box of shattered dreams. "We did all that work for nothing," Anya complained. "I can't believe it. What a waste!"

Nav was half asleep, but he managed to suggest, "We can still submit it."

"Like this?" Anya held up two broken pieces. "And say what, this is Big Ben after a Godzilla attack? That's our idea of an improvement?"

Nav didn't like seeing Anya so upset. He racked his tired brain for another idea. "Or," he said, "we could show the class our photo, the one that Kit took. We could talk them through it, and our teacher could still see our creativity."

Anya's unhappy face broke out in a smile. "Yes!" she cried. "You're amazing!"

Nav grinned. He was so tired that, for once, he didn't think about trying to look charming. He just let his grin spread across his face and felt really good seeing Anya's eyes twinkle. She was happy now, so he was happy, too.

Anya suddenly looked awkward. "I mean, good idea." She started walking faster.

Nav followed, still grinning.

A cold silence reigned in Lady Covington's office. Kit stood, arms folded, her face set in a firm Bridges scowl. Beside her, Elaine stood with her hands loosely folded and her body more relaxed. But she was gritting her teeth like she wanted to bite someone, namely Kit. They were waiting for Lady Covington to arrive.

"This is your fault," Elaine hissed.

"You threw Popsicle sticks at me!" Kit retorted.

"I was provoked. By your existence."

"Fine! I will stay as far away from you as possible in the future."

"An excellent plan."

Lady Covington came into the room and sat down at her desk. She folded her hands. She looked at the two girls before her with an almost restful expression. "Manners and etiquette can be quite subjective, can they not, ladies?" she finally asked them.

"Yes, Lady Covington," Kit and Elaine answered in unison.

"*Wrong!* We have a very clear and strict code here at Covington." The headmistress focused on Kit. "Miss Bridges, I understand that you are new to our ways, but you are beginning to try my patience."

Elaine couldn't hide a small smile.

"And I would be very careful if I were you, Miss Whiltshire. You more than anyone ought to know that that piece of theater the two of you performed goes way beyond the realm of what is acceptable here. And you—a prefect! I'm shocked and appalled."

Lady Covington paused to let her words sink in. "As punishment," she resumed, "Miss Whiltshire, you will tutor Miss Bridges and TK. I have already added them to the Rose Cottage roster."

Kit felt her stomach drop. That wasn't a punishment. It was torture!

Elaine's look of horror revealed that she felt the same way.

Lady Covington, of course, didn't care. "And I expect excellence, ladies," she finished, eying them frostily.

Elaine dared to speak. "Lady Covington, *respectfully*—she can't ride!"

For once, Kit was quick to agree. "She's not wrong!"

Lady Covington still didn't care, not one whit. "Well, then, this should give you both further motivation toward that end." When both girls remained in place, too dumbfounded to move, she snapped, "You are excused."

Josh had just started his shift at the tuckshop, and he was already bored. This was one of those days when nobody needed dental floss or a new school tie or a packet of peanuts to munch on the sly during deten-tion. He didn't need to do inventory, there was no new stock to shelve, and the price list was up-to-date. Things were dull dull dull.

He was halfheartedly tapping out the beat of his favorite song on the countertop when Kit showed up. He guessed that she had just left Lady Covington's office, where she had no doubt been chewed out by the headmistress for the Elaine-stick-throwing incident. Kit's expression was hard, her eyes cold, her body tight. "Candy bar," she snarled. "A big one. With almonds. I don't care what brand."

Josh picked out the perfect product and set it on the counter. "That'll be two pounds sixty."

Kit gave him the money and accepted her change. "Have you seen Miss Priss recently?"

"Elaine?" Josh shook his head. "You're the first person I've seen in the last half hour. If I see her, do you want me to—"

"Shave her head bald and paint it puce? Sure, go ahead. Send me the photo." She stalked away.

Josh sighed. He knew it was his fault. In a way. He felt bad, but he soothed the guilt by reminding himself that he may have set Elaine up, but she had deserved it. He'd had nothing to do with Kit's unfortunate involvement. The two girls had been at each other since they'd first met.

Still, he needed to apologize to Elaine somehow. He just couldn't think of how to do it without suffering major bodily damage.

No sooner did he entertain that thought than Elaine herself entered the shop. She, too, looked frighteningly angry, and she was glaring directly at *him.*

He decided to turn on the charm. "Hello, Elaine. Can I help yooo—ulp—!"

Elaine grabbed his tie and yanked him forward. "I just had a conversation with Peaches," she said in a low, icy voice. "Guess what she told me?"

"That her name is a fruit?"

"No! She told me that *you* told *her* to tell *me* that Lady Covington had invited me to tea. Is that true, Mr. Luders?"

This was the moment of truth. Josh nodded.

Elaine released him. "I knew it," she seethed. "Let me guess—*Bridges* put you up to it, didn't she? She thought I'd never know it was her if she hid behind you. I'm right, aren't I?"

It was a miracle—Elaine had it wrong! She thought Kit had set the whole thing up!

Josh considered his options. He was still miffed by the way Elaine had initially insulted him. And he was beginning to doubt that she was actually human. He said, "Look, let me just—"

"I was never so mortified in my life," Elaine said, interrupting him. "It was awful. That horrid cowgirl has no idea what she's done. I'm a prefect! What if the headmistress puts this in my permanent school records?" Josh was shocked by how genuinely over-wrought she was. Her eyes gleamed with unshed tears.

Okay, he definitely needed to apologize, but how? Elaine's idea of bodily harm was surely painful, if not permanent. Then he had an idea. "Oh, dear," he said in his most sympathetic tone. "I had no idea it was a lie, Elaine, *truly*. I thought I was simply passing along a message. Even so, my deep sense of personal integrity forbids me from disclosing or confirming the identity of the heartless individual who told me what I now realize was a cruel fib, but . . ." He paused for effect. "I'll tell you what I can do. How about some of our most popular makeup items, free of charge?" He sorted through some shelves and deposited several expensive items on the counter. "I mean, of course, free of charge to *you*. I'll make sure that the perpetrator of this crime pays for them."

Elaine blinked and looked at the items, speechless.

"But even this isn't enough to make up for your pain and suffering, is it?" Josh went on. "Let me add this!" He hurried into the back room and returned with a stylish sweater. "Just got it in. New for the season!"

Elaine's mouth dropped open, but she still said nothing.

Josh sweetened the pot a little more, just to be sure. "And one last treat." He set a box of fine chocolate next to the makeup and sweater. "This stuff melts in your mouth like velvet." He watched as Elaine considered the freebies. "I know this can't possibly undo what has been done, but might you accept it as their apology and let it go? I mean, you *are* the forgiving type, aren't you? No good can come from revenge—you know that . . . right?"

Elaine fingered the soft wool of the sweater, then let her hand drop. "I'd rather update her wardrobe with a hoof pick," she stated in a terrifyingly calm voice. "Have you seen her recently?"

"Nope."

Taking a step back, Elaine said, "You'll never let her fool you again, I trust?"

"Never. You have my word. "

Elaine nodded. "Very well." She lingered, still fixing him with her most evil stare, then snatched up the package of moisturizer. "That's for your involvement, Luders."

"Yes, ma'am."

Elaine disappeared around the corner, and Josh slouched in relief. He had apologized, in his own way, and she had accepted. More or less. And she was gone.

The next morning, Elaine gathered all the girls of Rose Cottage in the student lounge for a meeting. Kit figured something special was going on, because Elaine had put a guard girl on door duty. Every time Rose Cottage girls arrived, the guard opened the door, let them in, and then securely closed it behind them as if she were keeping out hordes of unwashed peasants.

Elaine began by handing out printed schedules to everyone—printed, bound, and laminated schedules, which made Kit roll her eyes. *Doesn't Elaine have enough to do?* she thought as she accepted a schedule and sat on the couch next to Anya. *I'm surprised she didn't use ancient Egyptian papyrus and dip the edges in gold.*

Elaine began to speak. "Today on the Rose Cottage agenda: preparing for our Guy Fawkes bonfire, to take place on November fifth."

"Who's Guy Fawkes?" Kit asked. "Oooh, I love bonfires!"

At the same time, Anya asked, "What's a Guy Fawkes? And what's a bonfire?"

They looked at each other and giggled.

Elaine was not amused. She passed out another printed, bound, and laminated paper: "The Complete History of Guy Fawkes and Bonfire Night by Elaine Whiltshire." The front page included an illustration of men wearing funny hats. "In 1605," she declared, "Guy Fawkes was part of a conspiracy to blow up the king, but he failed, and a bonfire was lit to celebrate. We continue this tradition each year."

"Probably, I'm guessing, without the blowing stuff up part?" Kit asked.

Elaine ignored her. "Each house will build their own straw Guy. The best design, to be chosen by Lady Covington, will be tossed onto the bonfire."

"Wait," said a confused Anya. "So you win the contest, but the thing you made gets destroyed?"

"It's an honor," Elaine said. "Our house wins ten points."

It sounded like fun to Kit. "Can we roast hot dogs, make s'mores, and tell scary stories?" She was kind of pleased to watch Elaine get annoyed. Kit was still miffed at having had a cup of Popsicle sticks thrown at her because a certain prefect had the self-control of a poked badger.

"There will be no *hot dogs* and whatever that other thing is," Elaine replied. "We will build a traditional Guy dressed in period clothing, just the way Lady Covington likes it. That is how Rose Cottage always wins."

"Always?" Anya asked.

"Always," Elaine confirmed.

"But what if we try something different this year?" suggested Kit. "We could try—"

"I have two more minutes for this meeting and no time for interruptions. Do you know why?"

Kit couldn't help poking the badger again. "Because they're coming to take you away some-where quiet and soothing?" Next to her, Anya snick-ered. Several other girls made little spluttering noises as they tried to suppress their own laughter.

Elaine lost it. "Because I am being forced to spend my precious time training *you* to ride a horse, something the rest of us had to master to even get here!" she yelled at Kit.

"Wow," Kit said, impressed by Elaine's blunt honesty. "Thanks." She wasn't pleased to have that particular bit of news revealed to everyone, but it would have happened sooner or later. Her pride could take the blow. She wasn't so sure about Elaine's pride, though.

Elaine addressed the group again. "Come prepared to work next time, girls. We meet again before curfew."

With the meeting adjourned, everyone began gathering up their things. Kit watched Elaine hand an envelope to a girl named Pinkus, instructing her, "Be sure this gets to Will Palmerston before lunch."

Kit whispered to Anya, "I think that if Elaine had her choice, I'd be starring as Guy Fawkes in this year's celebration."

"It'll be okay," Anya assured her.

Then Elaine's voice barked from out in the corridor, "Bridges!"

Kit decided the wisest thing would be to answer her master's call. It was going to be a long day. . . .

Meanwhile, in Juniper Cottage, Nav and Will were scrambling to get ready for class. Josh was in their room with them.

"We can't let Elaine win again," Will told his friends. "She'll be insufferable."

"I say we have our Guy built," said Nav. "Professionally." Yes, he had learned a lesson during the Big Ben fiasco, but the Guy Fawkes contest was more important than a class assignment. This was about house pride. This was about winning against Elaine Whiltshire. It was a top priority.

Will snorted at Nav's idea. "Built? By who? Ye Olde Guy Shoppe?"

"We don't need a professional, okay?" Josh said. "We just need a plan."

In his own defense, Nav stated, "I offered one, but I was ridiculed."

"Ridiculed?" said Will, putting on his tie. "That was nothing."

Josh stepped between the two. "Slow your roll, gentlemen. We're on the same team, right?"

"Fine," Will said. "I'm on the team."

Still feeling a bit stung, Nav said, "I'll be the captain."

"Dudes!" Again Josh stepped between them. "Who's got an idea?"

"I have a thought," Will said, slipping on his jacket. "But you guys would have to be ready for some next-level prankage."

Nav stared at Will, ready to do whatever it took, while Josh grinned. They were in.

Chapter 20

FAKING FAWKES & THE SADDLE PAD BLUES

Kit stood out in the practice ring with Elaine hovering over her shoulder and TK looking bored. She was dressed for riding, helmet and all, though so far, she hadn't managed to even get a saddle pad on TK. Kit wished she was back in the student lounge making Guy Fawkes jokes.

"No excuses," Elaine was telling her.

"I'm not making an excuse," Kit said. "It's totally a real thing." Referring to TK, she said, "He's giving me evil eyes. Oh, and now he's giving you the side evil eye, which means he's about five point six seconds away from doing his famous drop and dash."

Elaine looked across the field to the main building of The Covington Academy, sure that Lady

Covington was standing at her office window watching them. With binoculars. And probably a notepad, too. "At this pace, we'll be in uni before you get a saddle on him."

"Okay, relax. I'll try again." Kit approached TK with the saddle pad.

He stayed still.

Kit placed the saddle pad on his back.

TK reached around, grabbed it with his teeth, and whipped it off.

Kit couldn't stop from laughing. He was just so cute when he did that!

"It's not cute," Elaine told her. "We're being watched. Look, my reputation as your tutor is at stake here."

Kit turned to the horse. "TK," she said, making sure that her voice sounded nice and mocking, "Elaine's reputation is at stake, so you need to get it together."

TK snorted and made a long whuffling sound as he bobbed his head.

Kit turned to Elaine. "He says he's already one of the coolest horses in the stable, and he doesn't need your street cred to elevate his rock-star status."

At that, Elaine grabbed the saddle pad off the ground where TK had dropped it and proceeded to place it on his back. She'd barely straightened up before TK took off to the opposite side of the practice ring.

"I told you," said Kit. "Evil eyes!"

Without a word, Elaine dropped the pad over Kit's head and stomped away.

Kit stood there stupidly. She fully understood why Lady Covington had forced her into such a situation, but it wasn't working, and it wasn't going to work. Elaine didn't understand her and definitely didn't understand just how paralyzing her fear was. She felt like she'd been cast in some bizarre comedy routine destined for bad reviews.

She stood there with the saddle pad over her head, wondering what to do. "Is there anybody out there? TK?" She could hear the gelding's footsteps behind her. "Hello? Anybody?" Now the pad shifted on her head, no doubt TK's doing. His hot breath hit her in the face as he yanked the pad off. "Oh, so now you want to participate?"

She decided to try one more time. Gently she placed the saddle pad on TK's back. "There. Doesn't that feel nice? All cozy and warm, and it'll land you on every fashion blog."

TK yanked it off.

Kit sighed. It was easy to giggle at his antics when Elaine was there, but now that she was alone with TK, it was hard not to think of him being gone. For good.

What was she going to do?

Elaine left the practice ring and went straight to the main building to find a certain someone. She caught him between classes, walking down the hallway. Just the sight of him always made her stomach flip, but she was good at hiding her feelings. She caught up with him, projecting a happy attitude. "Hey, Will, did you get my—?"

"No," he said, handing back the invitation that Pinkus had delivered to him earlier. "I can't go with you to the bonfire." He didn't even stop walking.

"But we're a thing," Elaine said, matching her pace to his.

"No, we're not a thing."

"Yes, we are."

"We're not a thing."

Elaine's happy attitude turned sour. "We made it official before summer," she said, trying not to sound desperate.

Will stopped walking and faced her. "Elaine, yes, there was the end of the year dance thing, okay, but . . ." He shrugged. "It was a moment."

"But we've been in contact all summer."

"You've been in contact," Will clarified gently.

To Elaine's way of thinking, this was not a rejection. People simply did not reject her. She prided herself on being an accomplished student, and there was no doubt in her mind that she was destined for greatness. These thoughts bolstered her confidence, allowing her to stand tall and tell him, "No harm, no foul. I'm sooo busy with bonfire night to organize, and I'm tutoring that new girl, so I really barely have a minute."

"Yeah," Will said. "You must be jammed."

"Right. Completely. So, you see, as much as I'd like to, I just don't have the time to invest in a relationship right now."

"Sure. Whatever you say."

Elaine formed her lips into what she presumed was a pleasing smile. "I'm glad we got this sorted." She'd started to leave when Will spoke again.

"Bit of advice? Have TK follow you and Thunder on a lead. One horse will always follow another, you know?"

That was actually an excellent idea, one Elaine should have thought of herself, but all she did was nod. "Thank you for your input, but I've got it well in hand." She turned her back on Will and, wrapping her pride around her bruised ego, made a hasty exit.

She headed to the student lounge, where she found the Rose Cottage girls at work on sections of their Guy. "All right, girls, we need to step it up!" she urged them. "We will beat Juniper Cottage if it's the last thing we do. Patel," she said to Anya, "you're on wardrobe. Pinkus"—she pointed at her—"you're on straw. You—" She tried to think, but her rattled mind refused to cooperate. "I don't know your name, but secure a hat. Bridges, trot four lengths and end in a reverse."

Anya and the others gave Elaine a wary look. "Elaine? Kit's not here," Anya said.

Elaine didn't register her words at first. Her mind was racing so fast with so many things that had so many details, and her heart still hurt even though she refused to acknowledge it, and—

"May I make a suggestion?" Sally said brightly. She'd been standing in the doorway for only a brief moment, but it had been long enough for her to see and identify the problem. "Perhaps Anya could take over construction of the Guy."

Elaine laughed at the preposterous idea until she realized that Sally wasn't joking. "Wait. You can't possibly be serious."

"You're swimming in responsibility," Sally told her, not unkindly. "Everyone can use a hand once in a while, even you, Elaine."

"But I always supervise the Guy. That's how we always win."

Anya spoke up excitedly. "I promise to check in with you. Hourly, if I have to."

"But . . . but . . . I've got a plan!" Elaine held up the paper on which she'd drawn exactly how the Guy was to be built and dressed.

"Exactly," Sally said. "You've already planned it, and Anya will follow that plan to a T."

"Thank you, Miss Warrington!" Anya said. "The girls and I won't let you down!" And to Elaine she added, "We won't let you down either, Elaine. I promise."

Elaine didn't know what to do. She was so used to being the calm, commanding center of a whirl of activity, but now she'd been caught up in the whirl itself. And with all the girls watching, she couldn't exactly argue about it.

"That's settled, then," Sally said, pleased. "Back to work, girls."

Elaine watched her go, fuming. She thrust her Guy plans at Anya. "Everyone is to do exactly as Patel says," she instructed the girls, making sure they all knew who was really in charge. "Am I clear?" She waited until each girl nodded.

After Elaine left, Anya whispered, "I think we can make a few teeny, tiny changes to the plan, right? Just a few cosmetic things."

The other girls grinned.

Violet Cottage, where the First-Form girls lived, was under guard that afternoon. It wasn't an official guard—just Nav Andrada—but he was keeping a sneaky watch while Josh and Will conducted a top-secret mission involving unauthorized infiltration and acquisition.

He'd been there for only a few minutes, strolling back and forth and trying to look innocent when Josh and Will burst out of the cottage's quaint green door holding a Guy Fawkes dummy that sported a riding helmet and jacket. "Nicely done, gents," Nav said. They had their first Guy in hand. Now they just needed to steal the rest of them!

When Anya burst out the same door with something bright pink in her hands, Will and Nav blocked sight of their stolen Guy while Josh moved to intercept her.

"What are you doing here?" Anya and Josh asked each other at the same time.

Both of them answered at the same time, too: "Just hoping to run into that girl I like" (Josh) and "Just borrowing a blouse" (Anya).

"Which one?" said Anya.

"Which blouse?"

"No, which girl?"

Josh racked his brain for a name, saw the cottage sign by the door, and blurted out, "Violet! Her name is, uh, Violet."

"Oh." Anya thought for a moment. "I don't think we've met." She indicated over Josh's shoulder at Nav and Will holding the stolen Guy, which looked like a live person from her perspective. "What's with him?"

"Ummmm—"

Nav rushed forward with, "Oh, that's, uh, that's Nigel. He's, uh, considering Covington for his education. His dad's in Parliament! Though I'm not sure that's even relevant...."

"You know what," said Will. "We should be going now." He held "Nigel" as if "he" were about to faint. "Nigel has a rather delicate constitution. And he suffers from vertigo. And mumps. And, um . . . cataplexy."

Nav gave a sad nod to show how sympathetic he felt toward poor Nigel's difficulties, while Josh backed up, grinning for no reason except that he couldn't help it. "Yeah," he said to Anya. "We'd best be going." The three boys assisted good old Nigel down the path at a rather quick pace.

Anya knew something was up, but she didn't have time to wonder about it. She needed to make a clean escape with her pilfered pink blouse.

Kit was still out in the practice arena with TK when Elaine joined her again, this time with Thunder. Bringing Thunder along had been Will's idea, to be sure, but Elaine had soothed her ego by convincing herself that accepting good advice was a sign of superior intelligence. People like her became champions through diligence and hard work, but they remained champions by knowing when to take the good advice of others. Will might be a prat, as far as Elaine was now concerned, but he did know horses. "I hope you made some progress," she said as she brought Thunder up alongside TK.

"Maybe." Kit pointed to the saddle pad lying across TK's back. It had been there for several seconds—a record—but Elaine didn't acknowledge the success. Instead, she shoved a paper at Kit, who took it and read aloud, "'One: get TK to keep saddle on. Two: get on saddle. Three: ride TK. Simple as that. Got it?'" She turned to TK. "What do you think, TK? Got it?"

TK answered by reaching back and pulling off the saddle pad.

Elaine wanted to scream and stomp and pull her hair out. But she remained the very picture of composure. "We cannot fail," she stated as if it were a new law. "We'll be here all day and all night if we have to, but *you will get on that horse.*"

Six hours later, with the sun long set and the night sky twinkling with stars, Kit and Elaine were still in the practice arena with TK and Thunder. The two horses had been tethered together in the hopes that TK would learn from the other horse. When Elaine placed a saddle pad on Thunder, TK should have seen that it was no threat and allowed a pad to also be placed on him. But TK just wasn't getting it. Several saddle pads lay in the grass around him, and even Thunder was showing signs of impatience, tossing his head and grunting with annoyance.

"There's something wrong with this horse," Elaine finally declared as TK yanked off another saddle pad and tossed it down.

"If you were a little less rigid, we would be able to figure something out," Kit replied. She was tired and upset and sick of listening to Miss Do It My Way.

"Being rigid is what makes me a winner," Miss Do It My Way snapped, her own frustration leaking through. "Look, I can't have you scoring a zero, and that is the score you'll receive if you don't ride!"

Kit threw her hands up. "See? That stresses me out!"

Neither of them noticed TK pawing the dirt. Thunder tensed, eyeing him suspiciously and pulling against the tether. Both horses were catching their riders' anger, and both were tired and hungry as well.

"You are my responsibility now," Elaine told Kit as though speaking to a three-year-old. "You're Team Elaine. And Team Elaine always succeeds!"

"Fine," Kit said, "but stop pressuring me to ride or I won't. If I'm *afraid*, then I *will* get a big, fat zero!"

TK flattened his ears back and nipped at Thunder, who snorted a warning.

"Well, I won't accept that," Elaine said, folding her arms.

"Well, it's a legitimate problem," said Kit, glaring at her.

"Then solve it!"

TK lunged at Thunder, snapping at him, while Thunder kicked out angrily. Both horses strained against the tether that held them together, locking eyes and preparing to attack full-on.

Rudy sprinted out of the darkness and grabbed TK's lead, pulling him back with all his might while he disconnected the tether. Once free, Thunder scrambled back a few steps, neighing nervously, the whites of his eyes gleaming in the moonlight. Rudy pulled TK away, murmuring to him calmly and stroking his neck soothingly until the horse quieted. By now, Kit and Elaine were aware of their mistake.

"Are you two so wrapped up in yourselves that you can't see what's going on around you?" Rudy demanded of them.

"Mr. Bridges, we just—" Elaine began.

Rudy had no interest in excuses. "You almost had a very dangerous situation on your hands. That's enough for today. Go on."

"But, Dad, I—"

"It's Mr. Bridges right now." Rudy nodded toward the path leading to Rose Cottage. "Walk away."

Kit was usually impressed at how her father managed to maintain control of a situation while also remaining calm so that any nearby horses also remained calm. It was an essential trait for an equestrian, and something that both Kit and Elaine obviously had yet to learn. But when his calm voice was aimed at her in a reprimand, it hurt.

The girls exchanged guilty looks and silently headed for their dorm. Kit knew that it was beyond bad to leave their instructor (and father) to take their horses back to the stable, and she knew as well that this wasn't the last they'd hear about it.

Chapter 21

A HEAP O' GUYS & A MOUNTING SUCCESS

Anya was having a marvelous morning. The Rose Cottage girls had finished their Guy the previous night, and now she was on her mobile telling her governess, Madhu, all about it. "Then I said, how about a little glitz and glitter?" she chirped as she entered the student lounge. "And he's surely the best Guy England has ever seen!" She walked over to the chair where they'd sat their Guy down to dry overnight.

The chair was empty.

"No. Nonononono . . ." Frantically Anya checked the nearby chairs, couches, desks—no Guy! "Madhu, I have to go." She hung up and ran to the other side of the room, checking the chairs and couches over there. "Oh, this isn't happening! Where is he?"

Elaine chose that moment to enter the student lounge. "Where's our Guy?"

"He's just out for a walk!" Anya said before she knew she'd even opened her mouth. Pleased by the silly fib, she elaborated, "His legs were stiff. I think he maybe needed a little personal time?"

"Be real, Anya. I don't have time for your comedy act."

"I left him in the art room. To dry. I put a sign on the door. Nobody's getting in there—nobody."

Elaine stepped closer. "Then why are you panicking?"

"I'm not!" Anya said with a manic grin. "Not at all! Just sooo excited!"

"All right. See you in a bit."

"Good day!" Anya said as relief weakened her knees. "Sir!" she added for good measure. The Elaine crisis was averted. But—where was their Guy?

If she had looked out the window at that very moment, she might have found out.

Deep within Juniper Cottage, in Will Palmerston and Nav Andrada's room, a party of sorts was taking place. The room was filled with people! Most of them weren't real people, though. Most of them wore glitter and paint, and one even wore a pilfered pink blouse. Another had definitely been designed to look like Rudy, with a plaid button-up work shirt, toy cowboy hat, and work gloves. One wore a yellow construction worker's hat and outfit, though the reason for that was anybody's guess.

Will, Nav, and Josh joked around with their latest load of stolen Guys, which they had just daringly carried right across campus, in full view of the world. It was a minor miracle that no one had noticed what they were doing. They'd certainly been laughing loud enough.

They were still laughing. "Someone went a little crazy with the glue gun." Will chuckled, holding up a Guy covered in glitter and wearing a flower hat. He made the Guy wave.

"I quite literally have no words to describe that," Nav said of Will's Guy. His own Guy wore a black wig, a necktie, and glasses, which made him look like an office worker.

Will adopted an old man voice, and, manipulating his gaudy Guy to speak, he said, "My name is Robert. My mother picked out my clothes."

Josh snickered as Nav made his Guy respond. "Excuse me, sir? I've had complaints from other patrons. I'm going to have to ask you to leave."

Will's Guy responded with, "What kind of disco *is* this?"

Then Nav pulled out his mobile and took a selfie, including Will and their two Guys in it. "Blaaaugh!" they both yelled at the camera.

Josh got a very worried look on his face. "You guys are hilarious and all, but what if there's a bed check tonight?"

"Well," Will replied, "Robert here will distract them with some of his sweet dance moves."

"He could have a point," said Nav. "I mean, not Robert, the other guy—the Canadian."

Josh cocked his head. "Thank you?"

"Yeah, we might want to hide them somewhere a bit less obvious," Will finally agreed.

But where?

Meanwhile in the stables, Kit was leading TK from his stall. The previous day had been a disaster, but she was determined to keep trying to ride. Elaine wasn't anywhere to be seen, though. She'd have to start by herself.

Thunder lived in the next stall, so Kit told him, "Thunder, if you see Elaine, let her know I'm looking for her." She led TK out and headed for the practice ring, saddle under her arm and butterflies in her stomach.

The second she left, Nav and Will crept out of their hiding place at the far end of the corridor. Nav held a Guy in his arms while Will pushed a wheelbarrow filled with all the other Guys. Nav closed the stable doors as quietly as he could, and Will stopped his wheelbarrow near TK's stall. Then he fetched a ladder and opened a trapdoor in the ceiling. The hayloft was stacked pretty full. But there was just enough room for a pile of stolen Guys.

Working as quickly and as quietly as they could, Nav passed the Guys up to Will on the ladder, who shoved them up among the bales of hay.

Kit was beginning to despair. The morning had gone by, and still no progress.

"TK, come on!" she complained as he yanked off yet another saddle pad. "We're on the school's roster now, so we will need to ride together. A pad is barely anything! Plus, if we don't figure this out, you might get shipped to Siberia, where extra layers would come in handy, so you might want to work on it anyway. Plus there's Elaine's reputation to consider. . . ." As she spoke, she sneaked the saddle pad back on.

TK pulled it off.

Kit groaned. It was getting warm, so she took off her heavy jacket and absently tossed it onto TK's back since there was nowhere else to put it. She figured she would be warm enough with just her sweater. She bent down to pick up the saddle pad, and when she straightened back up, she noticed that her jacket was still on TK's back.

He hadn't pulled it off.

Kit gaped in shock, waiting for TK to do his grab-jerk-drop thing, but the gelding stood quietly, staring out into space, apparently lost in a pleasant horse daydream.

Kit looked out at the main building. "Is anybody watching this?" she muttered, wishing she could see if Lady Covington was at her office window or not. "Elaine?" Where was Elaine, anyway?

As if on cue, her cell phone rang. It was Elaine. "Hey, where are you?" Kit asked.

"Setting up for the bonfire," came Elaine's voice. "Debate Club ran late, then I had to race into a prefect meeting. Now I'm setting lights, assigning blankets— *Peaches, do I have to do it for you?*" she yelled suddenly.

Kit jerked the phone away from her ear at the shriek. Elaine could really holler when she wanted to.

"Anyway," Elaine resumed, "you need to complete what's on your list with TK today, and you'll have to do it alone."

Why am I not surprised? Kit thought. She was about to tell Elaine to march herself over and help her ride like Lady Covington had ordered her to do, but a much better idea came to mind. "Hm. Well, it is going to be hard for me to do it on my own. I could give it my all if I knew there'd be s'mores at the bonfire."

After a pause, Elaine said, "I don't even know what that is."

"Perfection! Graham crackers, chocolate, and perfectly toasted marshmallows."

"Disgusting," came Elaine's immediate opinion. "Absolutely not."

"Oh. Okay," Kit said. "I'll just tell Lady C that I'm practicing on my own this afternoon. I'm sure she won't mind."

Kit heard a distinct growling sound come over the phone. "Fine!" To some poor minion, Elaine bellowed, *"Get me marshmallows! Stat!"*

Kit clicked off, laughing. "Hey, if you behave, I'll share," she told TK.

Will quietly closed the hayloft trapdoor. All the Guys were now nicely stowed away out of sight. While Nav made his escape, Will set the ladder aside and had started to follow when Rudy's voice called out, "Hey, it's getting late. Get out of here."

Will nodded to his teacher, then caught a flash of blue on the floor. A couple of sequins must have fallen off one of the Guys. If Rudy saw them, he would know something was up, so Will casually placed his foot over them.

Rudy stepped closer. "You okay?"

"Yeah. All good." Will flashed a disarming smile.

Rudy left, shaking his head.

Will snatched up the sequins and darted out the stable doors.

"You, my friend, seem to confuse being funny with being stubborn. You're a horse, not a mule!" Kit was tired. At first she'd thought that TK's grab-jerk-drop routine had been funny, but it was quickly losing its charm.

"Nice outfit," Will said, strolling up to her. "Is that for the bonfire?"

"I'm not going anywhere until I get this guy tacked up. My time is running out!"

"Okay," Will said. "Let him smell the pad. That's normally a good approach. Let him have a cuddle with it. And keep talking to him."

"All right." Kit held the saddle pad under TK's nose. "Here, uh, here's a nice, cozy pad. Smells just like my jacket, dude. Same thing." She rubbed TK's neck with it while Will fetched the saddle sitting on the rails. "I don't want to miss my chance at my first genuine English bonfire night." As Kit said this, she sneaked the saddle pad onto TK's back.

Will took hold of TK's lead to keep him from reaching back and grabbing it. "And I don't want her to miss it either, mate," Will told the horse, "so get it together."

When Kit heard that, she looked up at Will to see what kind of expression accompanied such a statement. He wasn't grinning or anything. He hadn't said it as a joke. She blushed and smiled, making him laugh.

"Kit's been working with you all day," he went on to TK, handing Kit the saddle, "and now you're just being greedy. And that's rude." He kept TK's attention, holding the lead and patting his neck while Kit placed the saddle on his back.

Quickly she tightened the cinch around his belly and was elated when he didn't react. "You're such a good boy," she cooed at him. "Yes, you are. It's just me, buddy. Just me. You're fine. Nothing to worry about."

The saddle was secure. Will had already placed a small step stool at TK's side. Kit climbed up on it and grabbed the front and back of the saddle—which she now knew were called the pommel and cantle—so that she could pull herself up. She felt her heart beating too fast and had to take a couple of long, even breaths to steady it.

TK fidgeted.

Kit let go of the saddle and pulled back, heart thumping.

"Easy," said Will. "Whoa, TK."

TK settled. Will continued to calm him with long hand strokes down his neck as he nodded to Kit. *Try again,* his eyes told her.

She stepped back up and firmly gripped the pommel and cantle. Left foot in left stirrup. Pull weight up. Swing leg over. Sit. She was sitting in the saddle. "Oh!"

She was sitting in the saddle.

Will beamed triumphantly up at her while Kit whispered, "Okay, okay," over and over again, more to herself than to TK. She remembered to secure her other foot in the stirrup. She had barely straightened again when TK took a step forward. "I'm riding," she squeaked.

"I can see that," Will said, and placed the reins into her hands.

"I'm riding TK!" she repeated.

TK slowly began to walk.

Everything Kit had learned as a child about riding slammed back into her brain as if she had learned it yesterday. This was an English saddle and not a Western one, so she laughed inwardly, remembering how her first impulse as a child had been to grab the saddle horn. She couldn't do that now even if she wanted to! But she didn't want to. She just sat as a thousand memories washed over her.

The feel of *horse* beneath her came alive again in her mind, that marvelous shifting of massive weight as TK rhythmically alternated his legs to walk. She remembered feeling her little-girl hips tilt one way then the other, matching the shift of Freckles's weight as he had walked. She remembered sensing the awesome power in his muscles as his head and neck had nodded in time with his stride. She felt bigger in the saddle—she'd grown since her accident, and Freckles hadn't been that tall. TK was a much bigger horse, so the sensation of being a flea on a giant sea serpent came back to her. This time, however, she enjoyed it.

She remembered to hold the reins correctly and tried to keep her back straight yet remain relaxed so that her body could meld with the horse to make one smooth river of movement. A moment of faintness threatened to ruin everything when she chanced a glance to the side—the ground was *so far away.* . . . Mental snapshots flicked past her mind's eye: falling all that distance down, down, down, headfirst, her foot caught and twisted, Freckles galloping out of control, and her head bumping against the ground and pain and drums and thunder and—

No! I won't go there! That was years ago, and I'm an adult now . . . almost. And I will ride this horse, and I will love it, and TK will get to stay, and I will go to the bonfire in victory, and I will ride for this school and make my mother and father proud!

Will was laughing in delight, using his phone to snap a photo of the big moment. Kit glanced at him, and he gave her an enthusiastic thumbs-up. Her heart beat even faster.

"Okay, whoa, now I'm stopping," she said, gently pulling back on the reins. "Let's not go crazy."

TK obediently stopped.

Will moved forward to grip the bridle, smiling the biggest smile Kit had ever seen on his face. She refused to blow things at this point, and, controlling her urge to leap down and run away, she steadied her nerves and slipped her feet from the stirrups. Carefully, she swung her right leg up and over TK's rump until it paralleled her left leg, then let her weight pull her down until she landed on the ground safe and sound. "I did it!" she told Will, as if he hadn't been right there the whole time.

Will showed her the photo. "And nobody can say you didn't."

Chapter 22

S'MORE TROUBLE

It was getting close to bonfire time, but Anya had other things on her mind—like making another Guy. She had searched everywhere she could think of for the Rose Cottage Guy, but he had simply vanished. It wasn't her fault! Elaine, though, would never believe that, so her only hope was to build another one. In about twenty minutes. It was a totally ridiculous idea, but she could come up with no acceptable alternative.

Carrying a bundle of straw and her bag of art supplies, she dashed down the main building hallway and barreled into Josh. "Pardon me!" she cried without stopping.

"What are you doing?" he asked.

"Building an emergency Guy!"

"Sorry you have to start again!" he called after her.

Anya stopped dead. She turned around. "How do you know?"

"Oh, uh, I, er, umm . . ." Josh stammered, looking caught out. "You must have messed up the last one pretty large."

Anya's eyes narrowed. "Why would you say that?"

"No reason, I just . . ." Josh shrugged. "You know."

Anya's eyes narrowed even more. "How's your romance with *Violet*?"

"Great!" Josh said. "Yeah, she's great. Kind of chews weird but . . . um . . ."

Then he ran.

"Josh!" Obviously he was up to something, but Anya couldn't worry about it now. She grasped her armload of straw more firmly and resumed her own quest.

Elaine made one last tour of the refreshment tent. The bonfire was being prepared outside in the field, and the Guy judging would take place in the dining hall. The main party was going to happen in here, her domain.

Everything appeared ready as she strode between the long tables, double-checking every item. The white tent was enormous, completely enclosed from the weather, and brightly lit by an array of bulbs and fairy lights. She had placed the long refreshment table to one side, where it practically groaned under the weight of filled punch bowls and platters heaped with everything from caramel apples to biscuits to fruit tarts. Colorful balloons and Chinese lanterns added another layer of gaiety to the place. All in all, Elaine was pleased. Of course, there was room for improvement. There always was. But given her measly budget and totally incompetent "helpers," she felt she had done the best job possible.

The first student revelers arrived. She instantly took charge. "Right this way," she greeted them. "First-Formers over there—no, don't touch the food!" Why did people always go straight for the food? It was so impolite! "There will be a bell when it's time to eat. Thank you. Can you find Anya?" Elaine said to one of her helpers. "I need to approve our Guy."

The helper nodded and left.

Kit hurried into the tent with Will. She spied the plate of s'mores on the refreshment table. "You have got to try these," she said with a giggle, still high from her successful ride. Will hadn't stopped smiling since, either.

Josh sauntered up to Will. "Dude, can you talk to me for a minute?"

"Not now," Will said, but Josh hissed and gestured for him to follow. "Sorry, Kit," Will said as he left.

The second he was gone, the tablecloth over-hang parted to reveal Anya. She was hiding under the refreshment table! "Psst! Is the coast clear?" she whispered to Kit.

Kit crouched down. "Did you drop something?"

"I've totally botched this," Anya fretted. "I don't know what to do. Our Guy is missing! I looked every-where. I tried to make one, but it's a total disaster." She saw the s'more in Kit's hand. "Give me one of those s'more thingies. I want to taste one before I die."

Kit handed it to her. "What do you mean, missing?"

"Vanished! Elaine is going to kill me."

"Not gonna lie, that is a possibility," Kit said. "But who would have taken it? It doesn't make any sense."

One of Elaine's helpers tapped on a gong. The sound, deep and booming, filled the tent. "Lady Covington is ready to choose a winner!" Elaine announced. "Everyone, to the dining hall for the judging!" She headed out, grumbling to the gong girl, "Anya better have made a good Guy. Otherwise, she's going to pay for it."

When most of the students had left the tent, Kit helped Anya out from under the table. "I didn't know the end was going to look like this," Anya moaned through a mouthful of s'more.

"How's your last meal?" Kit asked.

In the face of doom, Anya managed a huge smile. "It's the best thing I've ever tasted!"

The two of them attacked the s'more plates, grabbing as many as they could hold. It was only logical to assume that Anya would need lots of sugar and gooey goodness to withstand Elaine's wrath.

Kit certainly didn't intend to end up walking beside Elaine as the students made their way to the dining hall for the Guy judging. She wasn't even sure how it had happened. And when Lady Covington appeared, stabbing both girls with a stare that could have stopped a zombie, Kit realized that she was being given a golden opportunity for revenge. *Oh, this is going to be great!* she thought merrily. *Elaine doesn't know I rode TK yet!*

"Miss Whiltshire," greeted the headmistress. "Miss Bridges."

Kit watched Elaine's pale face get even paler. "Lady Covington . . . exciting evening, isn't it?"

Kit could feel Elaine desperately trying to turn the conversation away from what she still thought was a failed job. She suppressed a grin, thinking, *Elaine probably wants to faint right about now!*

"I would like a progress report," said Lady Covington, "not about the exciting evening but about the work that you two are doing together."

Bingo! Kit thought. *Here it comes!* She kept her expression neutral while Elaine fidgeted. "Well, I . . . I tried—"

"And wow, did she succeed!" Kit cut in. "I got on TK!" *So there, Miss Perfection. I just saved your sorry bee-hind!*

As Kit expected, Elaine's eyes widened at this news. "You did?"

If Lady Covington noticed Elaine's shock, she didn't show it. "Really?" she said, pleased. "Well, of course you'll continue working together as it seems to be going so well."

Kit felt like reality had just warped. *Wait, what?* Her success was supposed to fulfill the requirements of the job and put a stop to this work-with-Elaine nonsense!

Elaine definitely thought the same. "Lady Covington, I really don't—"

But Lady Covington was already walking into the dining hall.

Sparks flew from Elaine's eyes as she scowled at Kit before following the headmistress.

Kit just stamped her foot. *Not fair, not fair, not fair!*

Kit slipped into the dining hall as Lady Covington was stepping up to the podium. "Good evening, students."

Everyone quieted down. Kit went to stand by Anya and Josh. She could see Elaine across the way, standing next to Nav. She really didn't want to see Elaine ever again, but there was no chance of that.

"I'm sure you're all anxious to get to the judging," said Lady Covington, "so without further ado, let us begin. Reveal the candidates!"

A set of long double doors normally separated the dining hall from the student lounge. These doors now opened to reveal a row of chairs. Each chair bore a sign with a house name on it. However, only two chairs actually contained Guys: Rose Cottage and Juniper Cottage.

The Juniper Cottage Guy wore a Bingham Academy uniform along with a gray wig, glasses, and a painted prissy female face. The Rose Cottage Guy was nothing short of an embarrassment. Kit had seen scarecrows that looked better. Poor Anya. She'd actually resorted to pinning her pink, frilly fascinator onto its bulbous, misshapen head. Its felt-tipped facial features seemed frozen in finger-in-the-light-socket shock.

A collective gasp erupted from the crowd.

After making a series of unladylike noises of

surprise and confusion, Lady Covington demanded, "Would somebody please explain the meaning of this? There should be a dozen."

Elaine had a stricken look on her face, as though she were imagining seeing the word REJECTED stamped across her future college application forms. "I'm dead," she moaned to the ceiling.

Anya winced, leaning in to whisper to Kit, "I'm dead!"

"Where are the rest of them?" the headmistress asked.

Having no one else to complain to, Elaine turned to Nav and fretted, "She's going to blame me."

Lady Covington said, "We're missing Violet Cottage, Alder House, Clover—"

"Excuse me, ma'am," Josh said hesitantly. "I need to say something. . . ."

Before Josh could spill the beans, Nav piped up, "Lady Covington! If I may, we've narrowed down the entries through a prescreening and voting process."

Elaine didn't buy it. "I call foul play!" Then she hissed, "Nav, what—?"

Nav said, "She can't blame you if there's nothing to blame you *for*."

"Excuse me, Navarro," said Lady Covington, "might that be a Bingham uniform on your house's Guy?"

"It certainly is, my lady."

"Goodness me. If I didn't know better, I would say that Guy bears a striking resemblance to Headmistress Branson." To everyone's amazement, Lady Covington giggled. She *giggled*!

Nav saw the opening and went for it. "What a coincidence that our Guy should depict our biggest rival!" He said the last part right in Elaine's face as if daring her to reveal the layers and layers of obvious "prankage" that must have occurred.

Lady Covington resumed her analysis of the two Guys. "Well, the Rose Cottage entrant is a bit of a dog's breakfast. I'm rather surprised it made it through your prescreening process."

Nav chose to say nothing at this point, while Anya looked like she wanted to cry.

"Juniper Cottage is awarded ten points!"

The boys from Juniper Cottage let out a collective roar, most of them probably just glad to have emerged from the judging alive.

Done with her duty, Lady Covington shooed them all away. "Off to your bonfire! Enjoy yourselves, though not too much, and remember the curfew does remain at twenty-two hundred hours. Sharp!"

The majority of the students had no idea what had just taken place, but it was over now, so they filed out the door in a rather low mood, suspicious as to where their Guys had all gone. The Juniper boys, however, whooped and yelled as they hoisted up their Guy and ran out at full speed to chuck the poor dummy into the flames.

Chapter 23

COMING TOGETHER

The Juniper Guy burned in glory as Kit and the others stood around the bonfire roasting marshmallows on sticks.

Josh insisted on taking an unthinkable shortcut: "You just stick it in the fire and then blow it out."

Kit wouldn't hear of it. "No, that's cheating! Respect the marshmallow. You've got to roast it low and slow, my friend, low and slow."

Josh shrugged and set his on fire anyway. He miscalculated when to blow it out, though, and ended up with an empty stick and a glop of charred goo on his shoe.

Over in the refreshment tent, Elaine sat alone, crushed by the Rose Cottage defeat. She should never have listened to Sally Warrington. She should have maintained control over the Guy project. Even more, she should have been the one to help that useless cowgirl finally get on her stupid donkey. Couldn't anyone see how hard she was working? Why weren't things turning out like they were supposed to?

"The evening's quite a success," Anya said, sitting down next to Elaine. She placed a plate full of s'mores in front of her, like a peace offering. It wasn't that Anya liked Elaine or anything, but she felt bad for having messed up the Rose Cottage Guy. Under the circumstances, though, she doubted anyone could have done better.

"All the planning . . . all the hard work . . . I just don't understand how this could happen. But I will find out." Elaine threw Anya a *don't mess with me* look. "Spill, Patel."

Anya knew what she wanted to hear, but there really wasn't much to tell. "When we went to get our Guy, he was gone," she said simply. "So . . . well . . ."

She grabbed up a s'more. "Eat this! You'll feel better, I promise. It's almost magical!"

Elaine glowered at the treat, the treat *she* had provided only because the cowgirl had demanded it. And of all the tasty goodies Elaine had arranged for bonfire night, these stupid s'mores were a colossal hit, and everybody was thanking *Bridges* for them. It wasn't right. Locating marshmallows at the last minute had been a real pain, but Elaine had managed it. Was anybody thanking her? Noooooo. And she had planned the Rose Cottage Guy to a T, yet they had lost! And, and . . .

Anya was still holding the s'more out with a hopeful smile. Elaine could smell the chocolate now, mixed with a whiff of roasted marshmallow sweetness. It did smell intriguing. Maybe she should try one, seeing as Anya hadn't really done anything wrong. She heaved a loud sigh, then accepted the sticky treat and took a bite.

She ate the entire s'more in two bites. Then she ate another one.

There was one thing Kit had learned to expect in England: rain. It had rained almost every day this month, though not always for long. Just enough to turn the ground to mush and force everybody to put on their mackintoshes. So she wasn't surprised to feel it start to rain down on the bonfire gathering. Thankfully, enough marshmallows had been roasted to make a mountain of s'mores, so everyone drifted off in different directions, seeking various shelters with their hands filled with them. The festive bonfire remained out in the field to burn alone in the rain, a symbol of survival in a turbulent world.

Kit and Will ended up in the doorway of the refreshment tent. They could hear the soft pitter-patter of the rain and could see the bonfire not far off. It was so big it would keep burning for hours unless the rain got heavy. Right now, it was just pretty to watch, a triangle inferno framed in the decorated doorway, bright sparks flittering about it like fireflies.

"I love bonfire night," Kit said randomly.

"Me too," agreed Will.

"Thank you for finally helping me ride."

"It's fine." Will held up his s'more like it was a glass. "Cheers." He bumped it against Kit's in a toast and laughed. Kit took a huge bite and munched as Will said, "We should do this again sometime."

"Yeff, iff woulf fee . . ." Kit laughed, spitting crumbs. She chewed until she could coherently say, "I've got my mouth full, sorry."

Will laughed at her. "You have made a bit of a mess. You've got some chocolate here." He indicated where by pointing to a corner of his mouth.

Kit wiped at the area on her face.

"And here," Will added, pointing to the other side of his mouth.

Kit wiped there.

"And sort of, like, all over here," Will said, indicating his entire forehead.

Kit swatted his arm. "Stop it!" She laughed.

"Honestly, though, you have got a bit there."

Will reached out and wiped the side of her mouth with his thumb. Kit's heart skipped a beat, and she looked up into his eyes. It was all getting so romantic . . .

She didn't notice Elaine farther inside the tent, staring at them, fuming.

Late that night, after everyone had gone to bed, Kit slipped her mackintosh on over her pajamas, pulled on her Wellingtons, and sneaked out of Rose Cottage.

The rain had stopped, but the ground squelched under her feet as she made her way down the path to the stables. Ever so quietly she opened the door just wide enough to squeeze through. She peeked into TK's stall. "Hey, buddy. You awake?"

TK grunted a greeting.

Kit opened the stall and stepped inside, closing the door behind her. She pulled an apple from her pocket and offered it to the gelding. "Here, I brought you a midnight snack." She held it so that TK could bite half of it, which he did, first tickling her hand with his chin whiskers and then gently plucking at the apple with his lips until he figured out where it was.

Crunch!

Half the apple disappeared. Patting TK's head, Kit listened to happy chewing. She had been drawn to this big, complicated animal from the moment they'd first met, back at the beginning of the school year when she had arrived fresh from America and he'd tried to gallop over her. She grinned, remembering how Will had frantically chased after him and how Nav had gallantly pulled her out of harm's way. All that had happened before she'd known Will or Nav, before she'd known anybody at Covington.

Now here she was with so many new friends (and not-friends) and a bright path to a future she couldn't have imagined a few months ago. "Wow, how things change, huh?" she said to TK. She offered him the rest of the apple. This time she put her ear against his neck. It was like listening to a giant chomp on a boulder in an echo chamber. "Nah, you're not scary at all, TK. Nothing here is scary. Just different, like I told Dad in the first place. Good different."

That made her think of Will and how she had actually been a little scared of him at first. "He's not scary, either," she said, feeling giddy. "If it wasn't for him, I might not have been able to ride you." She gave TK a hug, wrapping her arms around his neck.

TK lowered his head and tapped her back with his chin as if to say, "We're a team."

"Yeah, we are a team, aren't we?" Kit murmured, hugging him close. "Things are okay now. We're okay. We'll take this school by storm, won't we, TK? Just you and me, together. We'll get through this *together*."

She felt at home.

First edition 2017

Library of Congress Catalog Card Number pending
ISBN 978-0-7636-9439-5 (hardcover)
ISBN 978-0-7636-9835-5 (paperback)

17 18 19 20 21 22 BVG 10 9 8 7 6 5 4 3 2 1

Printed in Berryville, VA, U.S.A.

This book was typeset in Caslon 450.

Candlewick Entertainment
an imprint of
Candlewick Press
99 Dover Street
Somerville, Massachusetts 02144

visit us at www.candlewick.com